THE

CORSICAN BROTHERS.

CORSICA—PARIS.

TRANSLATED FROM THE FRENCH

OF

ALEXANDRE DUMAS,

AUTHOR OF "PAULINE," "CAPT. PAMPHILE," &c.

BY A PUPIL OF

MONS. G. J. HUBERT SANDERS,

PROFESSOR OF THE FRENCH LANGUAGE AND BELLES-LETTRES IN PHILADELPHIA.

PHILADELPHIA:

G. B. ZIEBER & CO., 3 LEDGER BUILDING, THIRD AND CHESNUT STS.

1845.

For ordering information, contact:

Buccaneer Books, Inc.
P.O. Box 168
Cutchogue, N.Y. 11935

(631) 734-5724, Fax (631) 734-7920
    www.BuccaneerBooks.com

PREFACE.

In presenting this translation to the public, I feel myself constrained to add a few remarks.

The duties of a translator are much more onerous and severe than I had formed an idea of, before commencing this little work.

It is not alone necessary to change the construction and idiom of a language, but in so doing, to avoid altering the sense or losing the spirit of the author's style; this fault in translations, it is generally admitted, is much more frequent than any other, and is one which I have been particularly careful to avoid.

Monsieur Alexandre Dumas is well known to the American public, as one of the most fashionable French novelists of the day.

His style is light, smooth and elegant; his descriptions of scenery and delineations of character, highly poetical and striking, while he is also peculiarly felicitous in witty and sarcastic colloquies.

The story of "The Corsican Brothers" is written in an easy, sketchy style, presenting on the one side an interesting picture of the habits, prejudices and superstitions of the Corsicans, and particularly of the "Vendetta," or war of vengeance, carried on between families and connections, sometimes for several generations; while, on the other, it gives a lively outline of the effects of Parisian life upon a sensitive and unsophisticated nature.

I have now in hand, and will soon present the public with the translation of another work of this agreeable writer; a spirited historical romance, highly interesting, and of much greater length than the present.

It gives me pleasure, also, to take this public opportunity of expressing my sincere thanks to Professor Sanders, for his valuable assistance; and dedicate to his notice, as a testimony of my approbation of his admirable method of instruction, the first literary effort of

THE TRANSLATOR.

Philadelphia, December 24, 1844.

THE CORSICAN BROTHERS.

CHAPTER I.

DURING the early part of the month of March, in the year 1841, I traveled in Corsica.

There is nothing more agreeable than a journey through this picturesque country. Embarking at Toulon, you arrive in twenty hours at Ajaccio, or in twenty-four hours at Bastia, where you can either hire a horse for five francs per day, or purchase one for a hundred and fifty francs. Do not smile at the poorness of this price; the animal which you thus hire or buy, like that famous horse of the Gascon, which jumped from the *Pont-Neuf* into the Seine, does things which neither *Prospero* nor *Nautilus* could do, those heroes of the races of *Chantilly* and the *Champ-de-Mars*. He will go safely over roads where *Balmah* himself would have used cramp irons, and over bridges where even *Auriol* must have required a balance-pole.

As for the traveler, he has only to shut his eyes and let the animal go; the dangers of the road are not his business.

Besides, this horse, who surmounts with ease all the difficulties and impediments of the way, travels on an average fifteen leagues a day, without demanding any thing to eat or drink. From time to time, when you stop, in order to visit an old castle, built by some *Seigneur*, the hero and chief of a feudal tradition, or to take a sketch of some old tower built by the Genoese, the horse quietly crops the grass near him, or takes the bark from a tree, or perhaps licks some moss from the rocks, with which he is perfectly satisfied.

As for the night's lodging, this is still more simple; the traveler arrives at some village, goes through the whole length of its principal street, selects the most commodious-looking house, and knocks at the door.

In a few minutes after, the master or mistress of the house appears at the threshold, invites the traveler to enter, offers him one half of his supper, and the whole of his bed, if he has but one, and the following day, while conducting him to the door, thanks him for the preference he has shown his house.

There is of course never any question of payment; your host would consider himself insulted by the most distant allusion to this subject. But if there should be a young female servant in the family, you may offer her a silk handkerchief, which will make her a picturesque head-dress when she goes to the fête of *Calvi* or *Corte*.

Should the servant of the house be a male, he will be delighted to accept a stiletto, with which, should an opportunity offer, he might rid himself of an enemy.

It will be well, however, to inquire

if the domestics are not poor relations of the master; this sometimes occurs, in which case they consent to accept for their services one or two piastres a month, with their board and lodging. And do n't believe that the masters who are thus served by their grand-nephews and cousins in the fifteenth or twentieth degree, are more carelessly served for that. No such thing. Corsica, it is true, is a French department, but Corsica is yet very far from being France.

As for thieves, they are unknown in this country, but there are bandits in abundance; they must not be confounded with each other. Go without fear to Ajaccio, to Bastia, a purse filled with gold, hanging down from your saddle-bow, and you will travel over the whole island, without having been exposed to the shadow of danger.

But do not go from *Occana* to *Levaco*, if you have an enemy who has denounced you as the object of his vengeance. I would not answer for your life during this short journey of two leagues only.

I was then in Corsica, as I have said before, in the beginning of March. I had arrived there from the island of Elba, had landed at Bastia, and bought there a horse at the price before mentioned. I had visited Corte and Ajaccio, and was now tráveling in the province of Sartene.

The same day I went from Sartene to Sullacaro; although the distance was not great, I had to travel about ten leagues, on account of the windings of the road on a prominent point of the principal line of mountains forming the back-bone of the island, and which I had to cross. I had also provided myself with a guide for fear of getting lost.

At about 5 o'clock we arrived at the top of the hill which overlooks Olmeto and Sullacaro. Here we stopped for a moment.

"Where does your signoria intend to take lodgings?" asked my guide.

I cast my eyes upon a village lying at the foot of a hill, and which seemed almost deserted; a few females only appeared in the streets, walking very fast, and looking carefully around.

In consequence of the hospitable custom of which I have spoken before, I had but to make choice of one among the hundred or hundred and twenty houses which composed the village. I sought to discover the dwelling which seemed to offer the best chance for comfort. My eyes rested upon a square, stone mansion, built like a fortress, with *machicoulis*, a sort of iron grating, before the windows. This was the first time I had seen these domestic fortifications, but I must also say that the province of Sartene is the classical ground of the vendetta.

"Ha! very well," said the guide, following with his eyes the direction of my hand, "we will go to Madame Savilia de Franchi's. Very well—very well, indeed; your signoria has made a good choice, and I see that you do not lack experience."

Let me not forget to mention that in the eighty-sixth department of France, the Italian language is constantly spoken.

"But," said I, "is there not some impropriety in going thus to ask hospitality of a lady, for, if I understand you right, this house belongs to a female?"

"Without any doubt," answered he, quite astonished, "but what impropriety can your signoria suppose there could be in so doing?"

"If this lady is young," replied I,

from a feeling of propriety, or perhaps, excuse me, of Parisian self-esteem, "cannot my presence at night under her roof expose her to observation?"

"Expose her?" answered the guide, evidently trying to give some meaning to this expression, which I had Italianized with the usual importance which characterizes us Frenchmen, when we conclude to run the risk of speaking a foreign language.

"Ah! certainly," exclaimed I, beginning to feel a little impatient; "this lady is a widow, is she not?"

"Yes, eccellenza."

"Well, will she be disposed to receive a young gentleman at her house?"

In 1841 I was thirty-six years and a half old, and I took great pleasure in giving myself the title of young gentleman.

"If she will receive a young gentleman?", repeated the guide; "well, what difference can it make to her, if you are young or old?"

I saw that I should get nothing out of him by this mode of questioning.

"How old is Madame Savilia?" said I.

"About forty."

"Ah!" exclaimed I again, always pursuing my own ideas; "that is very well indeed. She has children, no doubt?"

"Two sons—haughty young gentlemen."

"Shall I see them?"

"You'll see one of them—the one who lives with her."

"And the other?"

"The other lives at Paris."

"What is their age?"

"Twenty-one years."

"Both of them?"

"Yes, they are twins."

"And what is their profession?'

"The one who is at Paris will be a lawyer."

"And the other?"

"The other will be a Corsican."

"Ah, ha!" exclaimed I, finding this answer the more characteristic as it was made in the most natural tone.

"Well, then, let us go to the house of Madame Savilia de Franchi."

We then continued our journey.

In ten minutes we entered the village. I then observed a circumstance, which I had not been able to discover at a distance from the top of the hill. Every house was fortified like that of Madame Savilia, not exactly with *machicoulis*, the poverty of their proprietors no doubt not permitting this luxury in their fortifications; but the lower part of the windows were simply guarded by thick planks, provided with openings large enough to pass a gun through. Other windows were furnished with bricks. I inquired from my guide what these loop-holes were called here; he said they were called "*aretiere*," and this answer proved to me that the Corsican "vendetta" is of older date than the use of fire-arms.

As we advanced in the streets, the village took a more profound aspect of solitude and sadness. Several houses appeared to have sustained a siege, and bore numerous marks of bullets.

From time to time we saw through the loop-holes the glance of an eye, which observed us in passing with curiosity; but it was impossible to discover whether those eyes belonged to a male or female.

We at length reached the house, which I had pointed out to my guide, and which, indeed, was the most respectable looking in the village. One thing only struck me with surprise—the house apparently fortified by *machicou-*

lis, which had first attracted my attention, was in reality not protected; that is, its windows had neither planks, nor bricks, nor loop-holes, but only common sashes, guarded at night by wooden shutters.

It is true that these shutters bore traces in which the eye of an observer could not fail to recognize bullet-holes. But they were evidently of long standing, and had probably been there some ten years or more.

My guide had hardly knocked at the door, when it was opened, not timidly, with hesitation and only half way, but promptly, and in all its width, and a footman made his appearance.

When I say a footman, I am mistaken, I should have said a man. It is the livery that makes the footman; but the man who opened the door for us, was simply dressed in a velvet vest and pantaloons of the same material, and leather spatterdashes. His pantaloons were tied at the waist by a sash of spotted silk, outside of which appeared the handle of a knife of Spanish fashion.

"My friend," said I to him, "it is surely an indiscretion in a stranger who knows not a single soul in Sullacaro, to request the hospitality of your mistress?"

"No, certainly not, eccellenza," said he, "the stranger confers a favor on the house where he stops. Maria," continued he, speaking to a servant girl who came up behind him, "go and inform Madame Savilia that a French traveler calls upon her to receive hospitality."

At the same time he descended the eight steps, stiff and upright, like the degrees of a ladder, which led from the entry door, and took my horse by the bridle.

I took advantage of this kind invitation to ease and indulgence, one of the most agreeable that can be made to a traveler. I then undertook to ascend with ás little difficulty as possible the aforesaid ladder, and advanced some steps into the interior.

At a turn of the corridor, I suddenly found myself before a tall lady, dressed in black, apparently between thirty-eight and forty years of age, yet still beautiful. I immediately concluded that this was the mistress of the house, and I stopped.

"Madame," said I, with a bow, "you will find me very indiscreet; but the custom of the country excuses me, and the invitation of your servant has authorized me to enter."

"You are welcome to the mother," answered Madame de Franchi, "and you will soon be welcomed by the son. From this moment, sir, the house belongs to you—dispose of it as your own."

"I ask your hospitality for one night only, madame. To-morrow morning, at day-break, I shall have to take my leave."

"You are at liberty to do as you please, sir; but I hope you will abandon that plan, and favor us with a longer stay."

I bowed a second time.

"Maria," continued Madame de Franchi, "show the gentleman to Louis' room. Make a fire immediately, and bring up some warm water. Excuse me," continued she, addressing me again, while in the mean time the girl prepared to execute her orders, "I know that the first want of the traveler is fire and water. Please to follow the girl, and ask her for the things you may be in need of. We take supper in an hour, and my son, who will be in before that time, will have the pleasure, with your permission, of introducing himself to your presence."

"You will excuse my traveling dress, I hope, madame."

"Yes, sir," said she, with a smile, "but on condition that on your side you will excuse the rusticity of this reception."

The servant girl went up stairs—I bowed a last time, and followed her.

The room was situated in the first story, and had its windows on the back part of the house, commanding a view of a handsome garden, planted with myrtle trees and laurel roses; a charming rivulet passed through it, carrying its pure water to the Taravo. In the background the view was intercepted by a sort of hedge of fir trees, planted so near to each other as to have the appearance of a wall. Like all the rooms in Italian houses, the partition walls were white-washed, and ornamented with landscapes painted in fresco.

I understood immediately that this room, which was the one formerly occupied by the now absent son, had been given to me as the most comfortable in the house.

I then took a fancy, while Maria was busily engaged in making the fire, and preparing warm water, to take an inventory of the furniture of my room, thinking it might give me some idea of the character of him who formerly occupied it.

From the project, I proceeded immediately to the execution of my plan, by turning on my left heel, and thus making a circular movement round my own centre, which permitted me to take a view of all the articles by which I was surrounded.

The furniture was quite modern, a circumstance which in this part of the island, where civilization had not yet reached, I considered an evidence of a refined and elegant taste. It consisted of an iron bedstead, provided with three matresses and a pillow, of a divan, four arm-chairs, six chairs, two book-cases and a writing-desk, all in mahogany, and evidently proceeding from the shop of the first cabinet-maker of Ajaccio.

The divan, the arm-chairs and chairs, were covered with flower-printed calico, curtains of the same material surrounded the bed and shaded the windows.

I had proceeded thus far with my inventory, when Maria left the room, and thus permitted me to go further in my investigation.

I opened the library, and found there a collection of all our great poets: Corneille, Racine, Molière, Lafontaine, Ronsard, Victor Hugo and Lamartine; our historians, Mézeray, Chateaubriand, A. Thierry; our scientific men, Cuvier, Beudant, Elias de Beaumont; lastly, some volumes of novels, amongst which I discovered, with a certain pride, my *Impressions de Voyage*.

The keys were left on the drawers of the writing-desk; I opened one of them.

It contained some manuscripts, fragments of a history of Corsica, a sketch on the means of abolishing the custom of the vendetta, some French verses, and a few Italian sonnets.

This was all I wanted, and I had the presumption to think that I needed nothing more to form a correct opinion of Mons. Louis de Franchi's character.

I fancied he must of course be a peaceable, studious young man, and an admirer of French improvements and reform.

I then understood his reasons for going to Paris to study the law. There was no doubt a project of civilization in this pursuit.

These reflections I made while I was dressing. My toilette, as I had said to Madame de Franchi, though not lacking the picturesque, required some apology. It consisted of a black velvet jacket, open at the seams of the sleeves, in order to admit the air during the hottest part of the day, and through which *crevàs é l'Espagnole* appeared a striped silk shirt; a similar pair of breeches; Spanish spatterdashes covering the leg from the knee down to the foot, open at the side, and embroidered in silk of various colors, and a felt hat completed my toilette, the latter taking almost any form that I might give it, but most particularly that of a sombrero.

I was just putting a finish to this dress, which I recommend to travelers as the most comfortable that I know of, when my door opened, and the same man who had received me appeared. He came to inform me that his young master, Signor Lucien de Franchi, had just arrived, and requested the honor of welcoming me, provided I was visible.

I told him that I was ready to receive Signor Lucien de Franchi, and that all the honor of his visit would be conferred on me.

A moment after, I heard some one rapidly mounting the stairs, and my host immediately made his appearance.

———

CHAPTER II.

He was, as my guide had told me, a young man, between twenty and twenty-one years of age, with black hair and eyes, rather small, but admirably well made.

In his anxiety to pay his compliments to me, he had come up just as he was, that is in his riding dress, consisting of a green frock-coat, to which a *cartouchière*, pressing his waist, gave a certain military air, gray pantaloons trimmed inside with Russia leather, and boots with spurs; a cap in the style of those worn by our *chasseurs d' Afrique* completed his dress.

At his *cartouchière* were suspended on one side a whip, on the other a gourd.

Besides, he held in his hand an English rifle.

Notwithstanding the youth of my host, whose upper lip was hardly shaded by a light moustache, there was in his whole person a most striking air of resolution and independence.

He displayed the man educated for personal combat, accustomed to live in the midst of danger, not fearing it, but also not despising it—grave, because he is solitary—calm, because he is strong.

In a single glance he had seen all; my traveling-case, my weapons, the dress I had just quitted, and the one I had put on; his eye was rapid and sure, like that of a man whose life depends often upon a moment.

"Excuse me, if I disturb you, signor," said he, "I do so with a good intention, that of inquiring what are your wants. I always feel uneasy when I find a gentleman arriving here from the continent, for we are yet so uncivilized in our Corsican mountains, that it is only with trembling we extend, especially towards Frenchmen, that old hospitality which will soon become only a tradition preserved to us by our fathers.

"You are wrong to fear, signor," replied I; "it would be impossible to satisfy the wants of a traveller, more fully than Signora de Franchi has done; besides," continued I, looking round the room, "it is not here that I could complain of this pretended want of refinement, of which, with too much modesty, you accuse yourself; and if through these windows I did not observe this most admirable prospect, I could fancy myself in a chamber of the *Chaussée d'Antin.*"

"Ah! it was a mania of my poor brother Louis," replied the young man; "he loved to live *à la Française,* but I doubt if after his return from Paris, this poor parody of the refinement which he will leave behind, will satisfy and please him as much as it did before he left us."

"Your brother left Corsica a long time ago?" inquired I from my young interlocutor.

"About one year since, signor."

"You expect him back soon?"

"Ah! not before three or four years."

"That will be a long separation for two brothers who probably have never before been apart from each other?"

"Yes, and especially who loved each other as we did."

"No doubt he will come to see you before he finishes his studies?"

"Probably; he promised us, at least."

"At all events, nothing can prevent you from going to visit him?"

"No, I don't leave Corsica."

There was expressed in the tone with which he gave this answer, that love of the father-land, which looks on the rest of the world with a general disdain.

I smiled.

"That appears strange to you," added he after awhile, smiling also; "you are astonished that I don't feel willing to leave a country so miserable as ours; but I cannot help it. I am as much a production of this island as its green oaks, and its rose-laurels; I must have

my atmosphere impregnated with the perfume of the sea, and the exhalations of its mountains. I must have my torrents to cross, my rocks to climb, and my forests to explore; I want space—I want liberty. If I was transported to a city, it seems to me that I should die there."

"But how then can so great a moral difference exist between you and your brother?"

"You would add, and with so great a personal resemblance, if you only knew him."

"You are very much alike, then?"

"So much so, that when we were children our parents found it necessary to put some mark upon our garments in order to distinguish us."

"And when you grew older?"

"Then our dissimilar habits and pursuits produced a slight difference in our complexion—that's all. All the while locked up—all the time occupied with his books and studies, my brother has become more fair, while I, constantly in the open air, always crossing the hills or the plain, grew darker."

"I hope, said I, "that you will enable me to judge of this difference, by giving me some message for Signor de Franchi?"

"Yes, certainly, with the greatest pleasure, if you will be kind enough to trouble yourself with any thing of the kind. But excuse me, I see that you are more advanced in your toilette than I am, and in a quarter of an hour supper will be ready."

"Is it for me that you go to the trouble of changing your dress?"

"If such was the case, it would be your fault, as you have given me the example. But at all events I am in my riding dress, and I must put on my highlander's garments; after supper I have to take a walk where my boots and spurs would be very much in the way."

"You are going out after supper?" asked I.

"Yes," replied he, "I have a rendezvous."

I smiled.

"Oh! not in the sense you take it; it is a mere business appointment."

"Do you believe me so presumptuous as to suppose I have a right to your confidence?"

"Why not? I think every one should live so as to be able to speak openly of all his actions. I have never been in love, nor ever shall be; if my brother takes a wife and has children, it is probable that I shall not marry. If on the contrary he does not take a wife, I shall be obliged to do so; but it will only be to prevent the family from becoming extinct. I told you," added he with a smile, "that I was a real savage; I came into this world a hundred years too late. But I continue to talk, and at supper time I shall not be ready."

"But we can continue our conversation, your room being opposite to mine you have but to leave the door open and we can hear each other."

"You can do still better, come into my room, and while I am dressing, as you are an amateur of weapons I presume, you can examine mine; some of them have a certain value, an historical one I mean."

This invitation I accepted, as it enabled me to gratify the desire of comparing the rooms of the two brothers.

I followed my host, who opened the door of his room, preceding me, to show the way.

I thought I was entering a real arsenal. All the furniture belonged to the fifteenth and sixteenth centuries; the carved bedstead, with the canopy supported by large turned columns, was surrounded by curtains of green damask with gold flowers; the window curtains were of the same material; the walls were covered with Spanish leather, and around the walls were pieces of furniture supporting trophies of gothic or modern arms.

I could not long be in doubt about the tendency of the occupant of this room; it was as warlike as that of his brother was peaceable.

"See here," said he, proceeding to his toilette cabinet, "here you are in the midst of three centuries; look round, and in the mean time I will dress like a highlander, for I told you soon after supper I shall have to go out."

"And which among these swords, arquebuses, and poniards, are the historical ones of which you spoke?"

"There are three of them; let us proceed in order. Look at the head of my bed for a single poniard, with a wide sheath, and whose handle forms a seal."

"Here it is, go on."

"That is Sampiero's dagger."

"The celebrated Sampiero, the assassin of Vanina."

"The assassin? No—but the murderer."

"That is the same thing, I believe."

"In the rest of the world it is, perhaps, but not in Corsica."

"And this dagger is authentic?"

"Look at it! it bears Sampiero's arms, only the lily of France is not yet on it. You know that it was not until after the siege of Perpignan that Sampiero received permission to join the lily to his blazon."

"No, I was not acquainted with that

circumstance. But how did this stiletto come into your possession?"

"It has been in the family for three hundred years, and was given to Napoleon de Franchi by Sampiero himself."

"And do you know upon what occasion?"

"Yes. Sampiero and my father fell into a Genoese ambuscade, and defended themselves like lions; the helmet of Sampiero got loose, and a Genoese on horseback was on the point of striking him with his mace, when my forefather plunged his poniard between the joints of his cuirass. The horseman feeling himself wounded, spurred his horse and flew, taking with him Napoleon de Franchi's weapon, which was so profoundly sunk in the wound that he had not been able to take it out. And when my forefather, who highly prized this poniard, expressed some regret at his loss, Sampiero gave him his own stiletto. Napoleon lost nothing in the bargain, for this one is of Spanish manufacture, as you can see, and will pierce two five-franc pieces, one put over the other."

"Can I try the experiment?"

"Certainly you may!"

I put two five-franc pieces upon the floor, and struck them with great force. Lucien had told me the truth, and when I took the poniard up again, the two pieces were attached to its point, pierced through and through.

"This is certainly Sampiero's dagger," said I, "but I am astonished, that having such a weapon in his possession, he should have used a rope to kill his wife with."

"He did not have it at that time," said Lucien, "as he had given it to my forefather."

"That's true."

"Sampiero was over sixty years of age, at the time, when he purposely came over from Constantinople to Aix, in order to give this great lesson to the world, that it is not women's business to interfere with the affairs of the government."

I bowed in sign of approbation, and put the weapon in its place.

"Now, said I to Lucien," who continued his toilette, "here is Sampiero's poniard on its nail again, go on now to another."

"You see two portraits, alongside of each other?"

"Yes. Paoli and Napoleon."

"Well, near Paoli's portrait is a sword."

"Exactly."

"That is his."

"Paoli's sword, and as authentic as Sampiero's stiletto?"

"Certainly; for like that one, it has been given not to one of my *forefathers*, but to one of my *foremothers*. Perhaps you have heard of the woman, who, during the wars of independence, came to introduce herself at the tower of Sullacaro, accompanied by a young man?"

"No, tell me this story."

"It is short."

"So much the better, we have no time to gossip."

"Well, this woman and the young man introduced themselves at the tower of Sullacaro, and asked for Paoli. But Paoli being occupied in writing, they were not admitted, and as she still insisted, the two sentinels forced them out. Meanwhile, Paoli hearing the noise, opened the door, and asked who had occasioned it."

"I have," said the woman, "I wanted to speak to you."

"And what have you to say?"

"I had two sons. I was informed yesterday, that one of them had been killed in the defence of his country, and I have traveled twenty leagues to offer you the second."

"That is a Spartan scene, which you relate?"

"Yes; it does indeed seem like it."

"And who was that woman?"

"She was one of my ancestors. Paoli loosened his sword and gave it to her."

"Her? I like this way of complimenting a lady."

"Yes; it was worthy of both parties."

"And now, this sabre?"

"Is the one which Buonaparte wore at the battle of the Pyramids."

"No doubt it came into your family in the same way as the poniard and the sword?"

"Exactly so. After the battle, Buonaparte ordered my grandfather, who was then an officer of the Guides, to charge, with some fifty men, a number of Mamelukes who had continued to fight, keeping in their centre a wounded chief. My grandfather executed this order, dispersed the Mamelukes, made their chief a prisoner, and brought him to the first Consul. But while in the act of putting up his sabre, he found the blade so much hacked, that it would not enter the sheath; my grandfather deeming it useless, threw it aside. Buonaparte observing this act, gave him, in its place, his own sabre."

"But," said I, "if I were in your place, I would just as well like to have the sabre of my grandfather with all its notches, as that of the General in Chief, in all its brightness."

"Look on the other side, and you will find that also. The first Consul took it up, got the diamond, which you see there, inserted in the handle, and then sent it to my family with an inscription, which you will see on the blade."

Indeed, between the two windows and half way out of its sheath, which it could not enter, I discovered the sabre, hacked and bent, with this simple inscription, "BATAILLE DES PYRAMIDES, 21 JUILLET, 1798."

At this moment, the same servant who had received me, and had after awhile informed me of the arrival of his young master, made his appearance in the door.

"Eccellenza," said he, speaking to Lucien, "Signora de Franchi sends me to announce that supper is waiting your presence."

"Very well, Griffo," replied the young man, "say to my mother that we are coming."

He had just finished his toilette, and stood before me in his Corsican highland dress, with a round velvet jacket, breeches, and spatterdashes; he had retained nothing of his former dress but the *cartouchiere* which encircled his waist."

I was still occupied in examining two carabines, which hung opposite each other, and both bearing this inscription on the stock; 21 *Septembre*, 1819, *onze heures du matin*."

"And these carabines," asked I, "are they also historical weapons?"

"Yes," said he, "to us at least. One belonged to my father—" He stopped.

"And the other?"

"The other!" continued he, laughing, "belongs to my mother. But come down stairs now, you know that supper waits for us."

And walking out first to show me the way, he made a sign for me to follow.

CHAPTER III.

I must confess that while I walked down stairs, Lucien's last words, "this carabine belongs to my mother," occupied my thoughts very much. They were certainly calculated to make me regard Signora de Franchi with still greater interest, than I had done at my first interview with her.

Her son, upon entering the dining saloon, respectfully kissed her hand, which homage she received with the dignity of a queen.

"Pardon me, mother," said Lucien, "I fear that I have kept you waiting."

"In that case, signora," said I, bowing, "it would be my fault. Signor Lucien has related and shown me so many interesting things, that my endless questions have perhaps caused him to be too late."

"Be easy on that subject," replied she, "I have but just come down; but," continued she, speaking to Lucien, "I was anxious to see you, to learn if you had any news from Louis."

"Is your son suffering?" asked I of Madame de Franchi.

"Lucien is afraid of it," replied she.

"You have then received a letter from your brother?" inquired I.

"No," said he, "and that especially makes me uneasy."

"But how do you know that he is suffering?"

"Because, for the last few days I have been suffering myself."

"Excuse my never-ending inquiries, but that does not explain the cause."

"Don't you know that we · are twins?"

"Yes, my guide told me so."

"And that at our birth we were united at the side?"

"No, I did not know that circumstance."

"Well then, the use of the scalpel was required to separate us, and whatever distance may lie between, we form only one body; so that every physical and moral impression which is made upon either of us, has its counter effect upon the other. For the last few days, without any reason, I have been sad, morose and gloomy. I have felt violent contractions of the heart, and it is evident to me that my brother must have some profound grief."

I looked with astonishment at this young man, who asserted such strange things, without appearing to have the least doubt on the subject. His mother seemed likewise to have the same conviction, she smiled sadly, and said:

"The absent is in the hands of God. It is most important that you be sure he lives."

"If he were dead," said Lucien, calmly, "I should have seen him."

"And you would have told me, my son?"

"Oh! the very moment, mother, I assure you."

"Well then, pardon me, sir," continued she, turning again towards me, "for not having suppressed my maternal anxieties in your presence. You must know that Lucien and Louis are not alone my only sons, but they are also the last of our name. Please take a seat at my right-hand side."

"Lucien, sit down here," said she pointing to a vacant seat on her left.

We sat down at the extremity of a long table, on the opposite side of which were six other covers, for what they call in Corsica the family, those persons who in great houses hold a station between the master and servants.

The table was spread with profusion; but I confess, that notwithstanding I felt at that moment a most violent appetite, I merely satisfied it mechanically, my prepossessed mind not permitting me to indulge in the delicate pleasure of gastronomy.

It seemed to me, in fact, that upon my arrival at this house, I had entered a new world. I appeared to live in a dream. What circumstances could be connected with this woman, who had her rifle like a soldier? What, with this young man, who felt the same pains as his brother, at a distance of three hundred leagues? How could I explain the mystery of a mother who makes her son promise to tell her, if he should see her other son dead?

There was, you must acknowledge, in all this, sufficient matter for reverie.

But observing that my continued silence bordered upon impoliteness, I raised my head, and endeavored to shake off this confusion of ideas.

Both mother and son saw at once, that I intended to take up the subject again.

"And," began Lucien, as if he was merely continuing an uninterrupted conversation, "you concluded to visit Corsica?"

"Yes, so you.see; I formed this project a long time ago, and have at last put it into execution."

"By my soul, you have done well not to delay it longer, for in a few years, with the successive innovations of French taste and customs, those who come here to see Corsica, will find her no more."

"At all events," said I, "if the old national spirit retires before the advances of civilization, and finds a retreat in some remote corner of the island, it will certainly be in the Province of Sartene, and in the Valley of the Taravo."

"You think so?" said the young man, smiling.

"Because it seems to me, that all I see before and around me, is a very fine and noble picture of the old manners and customs of Corsica.

"Yes, sir, but notwithstanding, between my mother and myself, in presence of the souvenirs of four centuries, in this same ancient house with its pinnacles and gratings, the French spirit has entered to influence my brother; has taken him away from us, and has made him go to Paris, from whence he will return a *lawyer*. He will then live at Ajaccio, instead of living in the house of his forefathers; he will practice law —if he has talent he will perhaps be appointed royal attorney; he will then sue the poor fellows who have made* a skin, as they say in this country; he will confound the assassin with the murderer, as you have done awhile ago; he will, in the name of the law, demand the heads of those who have done merely what their fathers would have felt themselves disgraced by not doing. He will substitute the judgments of men for the judgments of God. And in the evening, after he has given a head to the executioner, he will imagine that he has saved his country, and think he has brought his stone to the foundation of the temple of civilization, as our *Préfet* says. Oh God! Oh God!!"

And the young man raised his eyes to heaven, just as Hannibal must have done after the battle of Zama.

"But," said I, "God has balanced all things well, for if your brother has become a follower of the new principles, you have at the same time adhered more firmly to the old customs."

"Yes; but who assures me that my son may not follow the example of his uncle, instead of following mine? and I, myself, don't I sanction things unworthy of one of the de Franchis?"

*FAIRE UNE PEAU, literally, to make a skin, means to kill a person in what they call an honorable cause, as for instance the celebrated Corsican *vendetta*.   T.

" You ?" exclaimed I, astonished.

" Ah, heaven ! yes, I, myself. Will you permit me to tell you what was your object in visiting the province of Sartene ?"

" Speak !"

" You came here with the curiosity of a man of the world, of an artist, or of a poet ; I know not, nor do I ask what you are. You máy tell us, before we part, if it be agreeable, or you may remain silent on the subject—just as you please. Well, now, you come here in hope of seeing some village *in vendetta*, to be brought into contact with some real original bandit, like those whom Monsieur Mérimée has pourtrayed in his Colomba.

" Well, I think I have then been tolerably fortunate, for if I have seen right, yours is the only house in the village, that is not fortified."

" This proves how much I have degenerated ; for my father, my grandfather, or any one of my forefathers would have taken part for one or other of the two parties which have divided this village for the last ten years. Well, and do you know what I am in all this, in the midst of the report of guns, the strokes of knives, and the blows of stilettos ! I am arbiter. You came to the province of Sartene to see bandits, did you not ? Well, come with me this evening, and I 'll show you one."

" How ! You permit me then to accompany you ?"

" Oh ! yes ; if it amuses you, it depends entirely upon yourself."

" I certainly accept your invitation with great pleasure."

" Your signoria must be very much fatigued," said Madame de Franchi, casting a glance at her son, as if she had partaken of the shame he felt at the degeneration of Corsica.

" No, mother, no, he must come ; and when in some Parisian saloon, they will speak hereafter before monsieur of these terrible veŋdettas, and of those cruel bandits, who yet frighten the young children at Bastia and Ajaccio, he can at least shrug his shoulders and tell them all about it."

" But what gave rise originally to this great quarrel, which as it appears is now on the point of being settled peaceably ?"

" Ah !" said Lucien, " in a quarrel, the origin is not of any consequence— but the result. If a fly, in crossing a man's path, has occasioned his death, the man is not the less dead for that."

I saw that he felt some reluctance to tell me the cause of this terrible war, which had for ten years desolated the village of Sullacaro. But, as a matter of course, the more reserved I found him, the more inquisitive I became.

" But this quarrel must have had an origin," said I. " Perhaps the reason for it is a secret ?"

" Oh ! no, not at all. The matter originated between the Orlandi and the Colonna."

" On what occasion ?"

" A hen escaped from the yard of the Orlandi, and flew over into that of the Colonna. The Orlandi went over to claim their hen, but the Colonna refused to give it up, claiming it as their own ; the Orlandi then threatened to take them before a justice of the peace. The old mother Colonna, who kept the hen in her hands, then twisted its neck, and threw it into her neighbor's face, saying, 'Well then, if she belongs to you, eat her.' One of the Orlandi then picked up the hen, and was going to strike the offender with it ; but at that moment, one of the Colonna, who, unfortunately, had a loaded gun in his hand, took aim at him, and shot him dead on the spot."

"And how many lives have now paid for this scuffle?"

"There have been nine persons killed altogether."

"And that for a wretched hen worth only twelve sous."

"No doubt the hen was the cause; but as I have told you already, it is not the cause, but the result which you must look at."

"And because there have been nine persons killed, there must be a tenth victim?"

"But you see," replied Lucien, "that this will not be the case, as I am going to be arbiter."

"No doubt you do so, at the solicitation of one of these two families?"

"Not at all, but at the request of my brother, who has been spoken to about this affair, at the Lord Chancellor's. Now, I ask you in confidence, what business have they at Paris, to interfere in the private transactions that take place in an obscure village in Corsica? I suspect the Préfet has played us this trick, by suggesting to them, perhaps, that if I would say one word in the matter, all this quarrelling would end like a vaudeville, with a marriage and a couplet to the public. They then probably spoke to my brother on the subject, who of course took it up warmly, and wrote to me that he had pledged his word for me. What shall I do now?" said the young man, raising his head. "Can I let them say at Paris, that a Franchi has given his word for his brother, and that that brother has failed to redeem it?"

"Then you have arranged all for a final settlement?"

"That's what I am afraid of."

"And we are going this evening to see the leader of one of these two parties, no doubt?"

"Exactly so; last night I visited the other."

"And is it to an Orlandi or a Colonna that we are going?"

"To an Orlandi."

"Is the rendezvous far from here?"

"In the ruins of the Chateau of Vincentello d'Istria."

"Ah! is it there? I was told that these ruins are in this vicinity."

"They are at the distance of about a league from here."

"Then we shall be there within three quarters of an hour?"

"Yes, in about that time."

"Lucien," here interrupted Madame de Franchi, "remember that you speak for yourself. You can make this distance in less than that time, as well as any other highlander, but monsieur will not be able to travel the road you usually pass."

"That's true;—it will then take us an hour and a half at least."

"You have then no time to lose," replied Madame de Franchi, with a glance at the clock.

"Mother, said Lucien, "permit us to leave you."

She offered him her hand, which the young man kissed with the same respect as he had done when he came in.

"If, nevertheless, you should prefer finishing your supper quietly, and then retire to your own room, to warm your feet and smoke a cigar—"

"No, no, no," exclaimed I, "diable! you have promised me a bandit, and I will have one."

"Well, then, let us take our guns, and *en route.*"

I saluted Madame de Franchi respectfully, and we started, preceded by Griffo, who lighted us out of the room.

Our preparations were not long. I put round my waist a traveling girdle that I had procured, before leaving Paris, which contained my powder and shot; a hunting knife was also suspended from it.

As for Lucien, he re-appeared with his cartouchière, a double-barrelled gun of Mauton's, and a pointed cap, a *chef d'œuvre* of embroidery, made by some Penelope of Sullacaro.

" Shall I accompany your eccellenza ?" asked Griffo.

" No, that is not necessary," replied Lucien ; " but loosen *Diamante ;* he will probably hunt up some pheasants, and we can shoot in the bright moonlight as well as if it were daytime."

A moment after, a large, splendid spaniel came jumping round us, barking with joy.

We walked about ten steps from the house—

" Apropos,"—said Lucien, turning back, " tell them in the village, if they should hear the report of guns in the hills, that we have fired them."

" I shall do so, eccellenza."

" Without this precaution," said Lucien to me, " they might think perhaps that the hostilities were renewed, and we should hear the noise of our guns re-echoed from the streets of Sullacaro."

After proceeding a few steps, we turned on our right into a narrow street, leading directly to the mountains.

CHAPTER IV.

Although it was now only the beginning of March, the weather was truly delightful, and would have been even warm, had it not been for an invigorating breeze which cooled the atmosphere,

bringing with it that peculiar fresh and acrid odor of the sea.

The moon appeared, clear and brilliant, above Mount Cagna, and threw a flood of light over the whole western declivity of the mountain ridge, which here divides Corsica into two parts. This natural barrier makes, to a great degree, two different countries of the island, which are always at war, or at least in enmity with each other. As we ascended, the gorges through which the Tavaro runs, gradually disappeared in the shades of night, the obscurity of which was impenetrable to the eye, and we saw spread out on the horizon the Mediterranean, calm and bright, looking like an immense mirror of burnished steel.

Certain peculiar sounds, distinguishable only in the solemnity of night, and which made no effect upon Lucien, who was familiar with them, produced in me sensations of strange and singular surprise, filling my soul with that deep emotion which gives the highest interest to every thing we see.

We arrived at a point where the road branched off in two directions, the one of which appeared to go round the mountain, and the other to lose itself in a path, hardly visible, leading directly to the top of the hill. Lucien stopped.

" Let us see now," said he, " have you a highlander's foot ?"

" The foot, yes, but not the eye."

" That is to say, you become giddy ?"

" Yes, the empty space attracts me irresistibly."

" Well, then, we can take this path which will not offer us any precipices, but only some difficulties of footing."

" Oh, as for that, I do 'nt care."

" Then let us go on ; this route will save us three quarters of an hour's walk."

" Go on, then."

Lucien entered first a small wood of green oaks, into which I followed him. *Diamante* ran before us at a distance of about fifty or sixty yards, scouring the woods on the right and left, and from time to time returning to the path, gaily wagging his tail and gamboling about, seeming to assure us, that we could rely with entire confidence on his sagacious instinct, and continue our journey in safety. I saw that like the horses of those would-be fashionables, brokers in the morning and lions in the evening, who use the same animal for the saddle and the cab, *Diamante* was trained to hunt bipeds as well as quadrupeds, bandits and bears.

In order not to appear entirely unacquainted with Corsican manners and customs, I communicated my observation to Lucien.

"You are mistaken," said he, "*Diamante*, it is true, hunts both man and beast; it is not the bandit he pursues, but the triple breed of the gendarmes, the voltigeur and the volunteer."

"How," exclaimed I, "*Diamante* is the dog of the bandit?"

"Just as you say. *Diamante* belonged formerly to an Orlandi, to whom I sent from time to time, while he lived in the country, bread, powder, bullets and some other necessaries of which a bandit is often in need. He was killed by a Colonna, and the next day I received his dog, who, being in the habit of coming to the house, soon became attached to me."

"But it seems to me, that from my window, or rather the window of your brother's room, I have seen another dog, chained in the yard?"

"Yes, that is *Brusco;* he possesses the same qualities as this dog, only I got him from a Colonna, killed by an Orlandi. Thus, whenever I go to see a Colonna I take *Brusco* along, and when I visit an Orlandi, *Diamante* accompanies me. If by any accident they should both become loose at the same time, they would devour each other. So you see, continued Lucien laughing bitterly, that men can reconcile themselves to each other,—make their peace, and go to the same communion table, but dogs will never eat out of the same dish."

"Well, truly," replied I, laughing also, "these are two genuine Corsican dogs. But it appears to me, that *Diamante*, like all modest beings, avoids hearing his own praise, for since we have been speaking of him, he has entirely disappeared.

"Oh! do'nt be uneasy about that," said Lucien, "I know where he is."

"May I ask, where?"

"At the mucchio."

I was just going to hazard another question at the risk of tiring my companion, when we heard a howling, so sad, so prolonged, and so lamentable, that I started with a sudden thrill, and laid my hand on the young man's arm.

"What is that?" demanded I.

"Nothing. It is *Diamante* making a lament."

"And what is he mourning for?"

"His master. Do you think that dogs are like men, forgetful of those who have once loved them?"

"Ah! I understánd."

Diamante here uttered another howl, longer, deeper and more melancholy than the first.

"You have said," continued I, "that his master was killed? we are then approaching the spot?"

"Exactly, and *Diamante* has left us to go to the mucchio."

"The mucchio, then, is the grave?"

"Yes sir, it is the monument formed by stones and branches of trees, which every passer by throws upon the grave of one who has been murdered. Thus, instead of disappearing like other tombs under the hand of that great leveler Time, the tomb of the victim grows continually, a symbol of that vengeance which is to survive him and grow unceasingly in the hearts of his nearest relatives."

A third howl now rung on our ears, but this time so near, that I could not forbear shuddering, although I knew the cause of it perfectly well.

In fact, at a turn of the path, I discovered at about twenty yards from us, a heap of white stones, forming a pyramid four or five feet in height. It was the mucchio; Diamante was sitting at the foot of this strange monument, his neck stretched and his mouth wide open.

Lucien picked up a stone, and lifting his cap, approached the mucchio.

I followed his example, imitating him as closely as possible.

When we reached the pyramid, he broke off a branch from a holm-oak, and threw on the heap first the stone, and then the branch, making with his thumb that rapid sign of the cross, a habit as truly Corsican as any, and which Napoleon himself made unintentionally, under certain terrible circumstances.

I imitated him to the last.

We then continued our journey, silent and pensive. Diamante remained behind.

In about ten minutes after, we heard this dismal howl for the last time, for almost immediately Diamante, with his head and tail hanging down, joined us again and renewed his duties as watchdog and hunter.

Meanwhile, as we continued to advance, just as Lucien had told me, the path became more and more steep. I

3

put my gun over my shoulder, seeing that I should soon be in need of my two hands. As to my guide and companion, he continued to walk with the same ease as before, and seemed hardly to notice the difficulties of the road.

After some minutes, climbing up the rocks, assisted by roots and bushes, we reached a kind of platform, overhung by some walls, in ruins; these were the ruins of the Chateau of Vincentello d'Istria, the end of our journey.

In about five minutes more of steep and still more difficult climbing than at first, Lucien, standing on the upper terrace, gave me his hand and pulled me up.

"Very well—very well indeed," said he, "you succeed tolerably well for a Parisian."

"That is because the Parisian you have just assisted to make his last stride, has made some excursions of this kind before now."

"Yes," said Lucien smiling, "I was told that near Paris they have a sort of hill which they call Montmartre."

"Just so. But besides Montmartre, which I do n't despise, I have ascended some other mountains, which are called the Righi, the Faulhorn, the Gemmi, Vesuvius, Strombolo, and Mount Etna."

"Well, now you are going to laugh at me, for not having ascended any other mountains than our Monte-Rotondo. At all events, here we are; four hundred years ago my forefathers would have opened their doors and bade you enter their castle; now, their offspring shows you this little breach, and bids you welcome to these ruins."

"This chateau has belonged to your family, then, ever since the death of Vincentello d'Istria?" began I again, resuming the conversation where we had left off.

"No; but before he was born, this was the residence of our common ancestor, the celebrated Savilia, widow of Lucien de Franchi."

"Is there not in Fillipini's work a terrible history given of this woman?"

"Yes. If it was daylight you could also see from here the ruins of the Chateau of Valle, where in former times the Lord of Guidice lived; he was as much hated as Savilia was beloved, and was as ugly as she was beautiful. He fell in love with her, but as she repulsed his advances he sent her a message that if in a given time she would not accept him for a husband, he would carry her off by force. Savilia appeared to give way, and invited Guidice to a dinner party. Forgetting, in the excess of his joy, that this flattering result had been obtained by threatening the woman he loved, he waited upon her at the appointed time, accompanied by only a few followers. As they entered, the gates were closed behind them, and a few minutes after, Guidice was a prisoner in the dungeons of Savilia's castle."

I advanced a few steps, and found myself in a sort of square yard. The moon shone through the crevices made by time, throwing long stripes of light upon the ground, nearly covered with rubbish. All the rest of the ruin remained in the deepest obscurity, shaded by remnants of the old walls.

Lucien looked at his watch.

"Ah!" said he, "we are twenty minutes in advance. Sit down; you must be tired."

We sat down, or rather laid down on a declivity of green turf, opposite a large breach.

"But," resumed I, "it appears to me that is not the whole story."

"No," continued Lucien. "Every morning and evening Savilia came down to the dungeon next to the one in which Guidice was confined, and there, separated by an iron grate, showed herself to the prisoner. 'Guidice,' said she, tauntingly, 'how could such an ugly man as you ever expect to possess these charms?' This torture continued for three months twice every day. But at the expiration of this time, by the assistance of a chambermaid whom he had bribed, Guidice succeeded in making his escape. He then returned with all his vassals, much more numerous than those of Savilia, took the castle by storm, and made Savilia prisoner. He exposed her in a large iron cage, at a crossway in the forest of Bocca di Cilaccia, offering the key of this cage to every passer by who might be tempted by her beauty. On the evening of the third day of this public exposure, Savilia was found dead."

"It strikes me that your ancestors understood the practice of vengeance tolerably well, and their offspring, killing each other merely with a gun or dagger, have no doubt somewhat degenerated."

"That is not the worst; but you will see the time when they will no longer kill each other. But, at least," continued the young man, "all that did not pass so smoothly in our family. The two sons of Savilia, who lived at Ajaccio, under the care of her uncle, had been educated as true Corsicans, and continued to make violent war against the sons of Guidice. This war continued during four centuries, and was finished only as you have seen on the carabines of my father and mother, of the 21st of September, 1819, at eleven o'clock in the morning."

"I remember, indeed, to have seen this inscription, of which you have not given me any explanation; for when I was on the point of asking you about it we were summoned to supper."

"I will tell you now. In 1819, there remained of the whole Guidice family only two brothers; and of the Franchis, there was left my father, who had married his cousin. Three months after their marriage the Guidices resolved to finish with us all at once. One of the brothers placed himself in ambush on the road to Olmeto, intending to intercept my father, who had gone to Sartene, while the other, taking advantage of his absence, was to attack our house. These plans were executed, but the result was very different from what the aggressors had expected. My father, informed in time of their designs, was on his guard, while my mother, also apprised of their premeditated attack, assembled our shepherds, so that when the double attack began, all was ready for their reception; my father in the mountains, and my mother in my very room. After a short fight the two brothers Guidice fell, one killed by my father, the other shot by my mother's own hand. When he saw his enemy fall, my father took out his watch; *it was eleven o'clock!* At the same time my mother, having destroyed her adversary, turned round to the clock; *it was eleven o'clock!* Their enemies had been cut off in the same moment. There was not a Guidice in existence. The race was extinct. The Franchi family, victorious, was hence undisturbed, and as they had bravely done their duty through four centuries, they took no part in new quarrels. My father got the date and hour of this strange occurrence engraved on the stocks of the two carabines that had served on the occasion, and put them up alongside of the clock, where you

have seen them. Seven months after my mother gave birth to two twins, one of which is your humble servant Lucien the Corsican, and the other his brother Louis the philanthropist."

At this moment, on that part of the platform illuminated by the moon, I saw the shadows of a man and a dog approaching. It was the bandit Orlandini, and our friend Diamante.

At the same time we heard the sound of the church clock at Sullacaro, which slowly struck nine o'clock.

Maestro Orlandini was, it appears, of the opinion of Louis XV, who established it as a principle that punctuality is a king's politeness. It was certainly impossible to be more punctual than this king of the mountains, to whom Lucien had named the ninth hour for their rendezvous.

As he approached we both got up.

CHAPTER V.

"You are not alone, Signor Lucien," said the bandit.

"Don't be uneasy about that, Orlandini. Monsieur is a friend of mine, who has heard you spoken of, and wished to pay you a visit. I did not think I ought to refuse him that pleasure."

"Monsieur is welcome to the country," replied the bandit, bowing, at the same time advancing a few steps towards us.

I returned his salute with the most minute politeness.

"You must have been here some time, already?" continued Orlandini.

"Yes, about twenty minutes."

"That's it. I heard Diamante's voice, howling at the mucchio, and about a quarter of an hour ago he came to meet me. That's a good and faithful animal; is he not, Signor Lucien?"

"No doubt he is good and faithful," replied Lucien, caressing Diamante.

"But if you knew that Signor Lucien was here, why did you not come earlier?"

"Because we had our rendezvous appointed for nine o'clock," answered the bandit, "and he is not more punctual who arrives too early, than he who arrives too late."

"Is that a reproach you make me, Orlandini?" said Lucien, laughing.

"No, sir—you may have had your reasons for doing so; besides, you have company, and it is probably on account of monsieur that you have this time abandoned your usual custom; for you, Signor Lucien, are also very punctual, of which, thank Heaven, I have received numerous proofs."

"This is probably the last occasion of the kind, Orlandini."

"Yes; had we, therefore, better not take up our conversation?" asked the bandit.

"If you are ready to follow me."

"At your service, signor."

Lucien turned back to me.

"You excuse me?" he said.

"Certainly, sir. Attend to your task."

They both left me and ascended the breach through which Orlandini had first made his appearance. They halted on the top of it, and stood upright, their black *silhouettes* strongly cut in the bright moonlight, which seemed to surround them with a flood of silver.

I could now observe Orlandini more minutely.

He was a very tall man, with a long beard, and dressed exactly like the young De Franchi, only his garments showed a frequent contact with the earth that served him for a bed every night, and of the briers in whose thorny mazes he lived, their proprietor, and through which he had more than once had to fly for his life.

I could not understand their conversation, on account of the distance, and also because they spoke the Corsican dialect. But I could easily discover by their gestures that the bandit repelled with great warmth a series of arguments which the young man brought forward with a calmness which did honor to the impartiality displayed in this whole transaction. At last the gestures of Orlandini became less frequent and less energetic, his language even seemed to become more peaceable, and after a last observation his head sank on his breast. He remained in this position a few seconds, and on a sudden impulse offered his hand to the young man.

The conversation, it seemed, was finished, for they both approached me.

"My worthy guest," said the young De Franchi, "Orlandini wishes to offer you his hand and thank you."

"What for?" interrupted I

"For having consented to be one of his witnesses. I have engaged my word for you."

"This alone is sufficient to make me accept it, without even knowing what the question is."

I offered my hand to the bandit, who did me the honor of touching it with the end of his fingers.

"So," continued Lucien, "you may say to my brother that all is settled after his desires, and that you have even signed the contract."

"There is then a marriage to take place?"

"No, not yet; but that will follow, perhaps."

A scornful smile appeared on the bandit's lip.

"Peace—yes, Signor Lucien, because you insist so much upon it—but no marriage; there is not a word said about it in the treaty."

"No," said Lucien, "that is probably only written in the future. But let us speak of something else. Did you hear any thing while I was speaking with Orlandini?"

"Of your conversation, you mean?"

"No—but of a pheasant, who was also talking somewhere about here?"

"It seemed to me, indeed, that I heard the voice of a bird; but I thought I was mistaken."

"No, you were not mistaken," said the bandit; "there is a cock-pheasant sitting in the great chestnut tree, about a hundred yards from here. I heard him a little while ago."

"Well," said Lucien, merrily, "we must have him for our dinner to-morrow."

"I should have brought him down long ago," said Orlandini, "had I not been afraid they might have thought in the village that I was hunting other game than pheasants."

"Apropos," continued he, putting his gun over his shoulder, which he was just getting ready, "you shall have that honor, monsieur."

"Excuse me, sir; I am not as sure of my aim as you are, but I am as deeply interested in eating my part of the pheasant to-morrow, as you are in shooting him."

"The fact is," said Lucien, "you are not accustomed, as we are, to hunting after night, and you would certainly shoot too low; besides, if you have nothing better to do to-morrow, you may then take your turn."

We stepped out of the ruins on the side opposite that by which we had entered. Lucien went first, and he had hardly set his foot in the thicket before we heard the pheasant calling again. It was about eighty steps from us, hid by the branches of a large chestnut tree, surrounded on all sides by thick underwood.

"But how in the world will you approach without alarming him?" inquired I; "it does not appear to me to be very easy."

"If I could only see him," said Lucien, "I could shoot him from here."

"How? from here? Have you a gun that will kill pheasants at eighty steps distance?"

"With shot—no. With a bullet—yes."

"With a bullet? Ah, enough then—that's another thing. You have done very well not to let me shoot."

"Would you like to see the pheasant?" asked Orlandini.

"Certainly—it would give me great pleasure."

"Wait a moment."

And Orlandini began to imitate the clucking of the hen-pheasant.

At the same moment, without perceiving the bird, we heard a rustling among the leaves of the chestnut tree; the pheasant ascended from branch to branch, all the time answering by his cries the treacherous advances made by Orlandini, until at last he appeared on the top of the tree, perfectly visible, showing a dark outline on the bluish white of the sky.

Orlandini kept silence—the pheasant remained without moving, and at the same time Lucien took aim at him and shot.

The pheasant came down like a ball.

"Go seek!" said Lucien to Diamante, who sprung into the bushes, and in a few minutes returned with the pheasant in his mouth.

The bullet had gone through its body.

"I must compliment you upon that shot," said I, "particularly as it was done with a double-barreled gun."

"Oh," replied Lucien, "there is not so much merit in it as you think; one of the barrels being rifled carries the bullet like a carabine."

"No matter—even with a carabine the shot would deserve a favorable mention."

"Bah!" said Orlandini, "with a carabine Signor Lucien can strike a five-franc piece at three hundred steps distance."

"And do you shoot equally well with a pistol?"

"Nearly so," replied Lucien; "at twenty-five steps distance I always cut in two, six bullets out of twelve, on the blade of a knife."

I raised my hat and bowed to Lucien.

"And your brother," said I, "is he as good a shot as you are?"

"My brother? Poor Louis! he has never touched a gun or pistol in his life; and I am always afraid he may get into some bad affair at Paris; for, brave as he is, he would expose himself to certain death in maintaining the honor of his country."

Lucien put the pheasant in the wide pocket of his velvet jacket.

"Now, my dear Orlandini," continued he, "till to-morrow! I know your punctuality! At 10 o'clock you will be at the extremity of the street, with your friends and relations from the hill-side; at the same time, on the opposite side of the street, Colonna, on his part, will arrive with his relations and friends. As for us, you will see us on the steps of the church."

"All right, Signor Lucien—thank you for the trouble; and to you, sir," continued Orlandini, turning to me and bowing, "thank you for the honor."

After this exchange of compliments, we separated; Orlandini disappeared in the thicket, and we took the road to the village.

As for Diamante, he seemed for some moments undecided between Orlandini and ourselves; he looked alternately to the right and left, but after some hesitation favored us with the preference.

I confess that when I ascended these steep, wild rocks, I had felt some uneasiness about the way of getting down again, for it is a well known fact that it is much easier to ascend than to descend. I saw, therefore, with pleasure, Lucien taking another road, he probably guessing my apprehensions on the subject.

This road afforded me the additional enjoyment of conversation, which in all steep and difficult places must naturally be interrupted. Here, the declivity being gradual and the road easy, we had not proceeded more than fifty steps when I recommenced my interrogatories.

"Then peace is concluded now?"

"Yes; but as you have seen, not without difficulty. I have convinced him that all advances have been made by the Colonna. First, they have had five persons killed, while the Colonna have had only four men sacrificed. The Colonna had already yesterday consented to the reconciliation, while the Orlandini have given theirs only to-day. Lastly, the Colonna have engaged themselves to return, publicly, a living hen, to the Orlandini; a concession which is a proof that they acknowledge themselves to have been in the wrong. This last consideration decided him."

" And this interesting reconciliation is to take place to-morrow ?"

" At ten o'clock. You see you have not been so unlucky after all. You hoped to see a vendetta ? Bah ! what would that have been ? For four hundred years there has been nothing else spoken of in Corsica, but a reconciliation ! That 's much more extraordinary !"

I could not help smiling.

" You laugh at us now," continued he ; " well, you are right—we are, in fact, a curious people."

" No," said I, " I laugh only at the inconsistency of seeing you so furious against yourself, for having been successful."

" Ah, sir ! if you had been able to understand me, you would have admired my eloquence. But call again in ten years, and every body will speak French here."

" You are an excellent lawyer."

" No, no—understand me ! I am only an arbiter. How can I help it ? Is it not the duty of an arbiter to reconcile ? If I were appointed arbiter between God and Satan, I should certainly try to reconcile them ; but in the depths of my heart I should think it very foolish for God to listen to me."

Seeing that this topic of conversation had no other effect than to irritate my companion, I remained silent, and as he did not resume it, we reached home without exchanging another word.

———

CHAPTER VI.

Griffo was waiting for us. Even before his master spoke to him, he began to search the pocket of his jacket, and drew out the pheasant. He had heard and recognized the report of his gun.

Madame de Franchi was not yet asleep, she had only retired to her room, leaving orders with Griffo, to request her son to call upon her before going to bed.

The young man inquired if I wanted any thing, and upon my answering in the negative, asked my leave to wait on his mother.

I gave him that permission with great pleasure, and retired to my own room. I entered with a certain pride. My studies on analogies had not misled me, and I was glad to have so correctly guessed the character of Louis, as I should also have divined that of Lucien. I undressed slowly, and after having chosen from the future lawyer's library, the " *Orientales*," by Victor Hugo, I laid down filled with self satisfaction.

I had just read, for the hundredth time, the *Feu du Ciel* when I heard footsteps on the stairs, which soon halted softly at my door. I suspected it was my host, who came with the intention of bidding me good night, but hesitated to open the door, not knowing whether I was asleep or not.

" Come in !" said I, putting my book on the night table.

The door opened, and Lucien entered.

" Excuse me," said he, " but upon reflection, it seemed to me that I had been so taciturn this evening, that I could not go to bed without asking your pardon. I therefore come here to make the *amende honorable*, and as you appear to have a great many questions on hand, I put myself now at your service."

" A thousand thanks, said I. On the contrary, through your kindness I am informed of nearly every thing I wished to know. There is but one thing left to excite my curiosity, but which I have made up my mind not to question you about."

"Why not?"

"That would be truly a great indiscretion. But pray, do n't urge me, for I cannot guarantee my reserve."

"Well, go on then: an unsatisfied curiosity is a very bad thing. It naturally awakens conjectures, and out of three conjectures there are always two, at least, more hurtful to the interested person, than the truth would be."

"Be easy on that subject. My most injurious suspicions against you lead me simply to believe you to be a kind of sorcerer."

The young man smiled.

"Diable," said he, "you now make me as curious as you are; pray explain yourself."

"Well! you have been kind enough to clear up all that was obscure to me, with the exception of only one point. You have shown me those beautiful historical weapons,—which, by the by, I shall ask the permission to see again before I leave."

"That 's one!"

"You have explained the meaning of the double inscription on the stock of those two carabines."

"Makes two! go on."

"You havé informed me how, agreeably to the phenomenon of your birth, you feel, at three hundred leagues distance, the same emotions as your brother, who, in his turn no doubt, feels yours."

"Makes three!"

"But when Madame de Franchi, in speaking of the sad feeling which gave you a presentiment that something disagreeable had occurred to your brother, when," said I, "she asked you, if you were sure that he was not dead, you answered her, no! if he were dead I should have seen him——"

"Yes, that was my answer to her."

"Well, if the explanation of these words be permitted to enter a profane ear, I pray you give it to me."

As I spoke, the face of the young man gradually took so grave an expression, that I pronounced the last words with some hesitation. There was, even after I had finished speaking, a momentary silence between us.

"I feel that I have been indiscreet," said I; "excuse me, and let us suppose that I have not said any thing on this subject."

"No," replied he, "only you are a man of the world, and, consequently, a little incredulous. I therefore fear that you will consider, as an idle superstition, an old family tradition, which has existed now amongst us for four hundred years."

"Listen, sir, if you please; I swear to you, that in respect to legends and traditions, nobody can be more credulous than myself; there are even things of this kind, which I believe implicitly; I mean impossibilities."

"So you believe in apparitions?"

"Will you permit me to relate what happened to myself?"

"Yes, that will encourage me."

"My father died in 1807, consequently, at that time I was only about three years and a half old. As the physicians had declared that my suffering parent could not survive very long, I was sent to an old cousin who lived in a house situated between a yard and a garden. She had prepared a bed for me opposite hers, where she placed me at the usual hour. In spite of the misfortune which was about to befall me, and of which, by the by, I was totally unconscious, I fell asleep. Suddenly three violent and hurried knocks were heard at the door. I sprang out of bed and approached the door.

"Where are you going!" cried my cousin, who, like me, awakened by the noise of the three blows, could not suppress a certain degree of terror, knowing that the principal entry door of the street being locked, nobody could enter to knock at the door of our bedchamber.

"I am going to admit papa, who comes to bid me farewell," said I.

She then got up and put me to bed again; but I resisted, crying very much and exclaiming,—"Papa is at the door, and I must see papa before he leaves me forever."

"Has that apparition ever made its appearance since that time?"

"No, though I have recalled it often enough. But God, perhaps, grants to a child's purity, privileges which are refused to man's corrupt nature."

"Then," said Lucien, smiling, "we are more fortunate in our family than you are."

"Have your deceased ancestors ever shown themselves?"

"Each time that a great event is about to take place."

"And to what do you attribute this privilege being granted to your family?"

"I am going to give you the whole tradition, such as we have preserved it. I told you that Savilia died, leaving two sons."

"Yes, I recollect that."

"These two sons grew up, in an attachment the most devoted, concentrating upon each other all the affection and tenderness which would have been shared with their relatives, if they had lived. They swore to each other, that nothing, not even death, should separate them: and by the aid of I know not what powerful conjuration, they wrote with their blood on a piece of parchment the reciprocal oath, that he who died first, should appear to the other at the moment of his death, and in every time of great extremity during his life. Three months after, one of the brothers was killed in an ambuscade, in the very moment when the other brother was sealing a letter written to him. As he was putting his seal on the hot wax, he heard a sigh behind him, and, turning round, he saw his brother standing there, leaning with his hand resting upon his shoulder, although he felt no weight, nor even the impression of his hand. By a mechanical impulse he presented the letter to his brother, who took it and disappeared. The night before he died he saw this apparition again.

"Without doubt, the two brothers had not only pledged their word for themselves, but also for their offspring, for since that time the apparitions have appeared not only at the time when a death was about to take place, but also upon the eve of all great events connected with the family."

"And have you ever had a vision of this kind?"

"No; but as my father, during the night preceding his death, was informed by his brother of his approaching end, I presume that my brother and I shall enjoy the privilege of our ancestors, as we have never done any thing to make us unworthy of that favor."

"And this privilege is only granted to the males of the family?"

"Yes."

"That's strange."

"So it is."

I looked at the young man, who, cold, grave and calm, told me a thing considered impossible, and I repeated with Hamlet—

"There are more things in heaven and earth, Horatio,
Than are dreamt of in your philosophy!'

At Paris, I would have considered the young man as a mystifier; but in the heart of Corsica, in a little obscure village, I was constrained to look upon him as a fool who believed implicitly in the deceptions of his imagination, or a being more or less fortunate than other people.

" And now," said he, after a long pause, "have I told you all you wished to know?"

"Yes, I thank you, I am much gratified at your confidence in me, and I promise you to keep it secret."

"Oh!" replied he, smiling, "there is no secret in all this, and the first peasant you might meet in the village, would have told you the same story. I only hope that my brother may not have boasted at Paris of this privilege; the consequence would probably be, that the men would laugh in his face, and the women get a nervous attack."

After these words he got up, and wishing me good night, retired to his chamber.

"Notwithstanding my fatigue, it was some time before I could go to sleep, and even then my rest was disturbed and agitated. I saw confusedly in my dreams all the persons with whom I had had any intercourse during the day, but all was without order or connection. Towards daylight only, I fell into a sound sleep, and did not wake until the pealing of the church bell resounded in my ears.

I rung my bell, for my luxurious predecessor had carried his love of ease so far, as to have within reach of his hand the string of a bell, the only one of the kind, no doubt, existing in the village.

Griffo came up immediately with warm water. I saw that Signor Louis de Franchi had trained this valet-de-chambre tolerably well.

Lucien had already twice asked if I was up, declaring that if at half past nine I was not awake, he would come into my room.

It was twenty-five minutes past nine, and so, he soon after made his appearance.

He was dressed in the French style, and even in the style of the French *élégant*. He had on a black frock coat, a vest *de fantaisie*, and a pair of white pantaloons, for even in the beginning of March, white pantaloons were quite seasonable in Corsica.

He observed that I was looking at him with some degree of astonishment.

" You admire my dress, said he; "this is a new proof of my progress in civilization."

"Yes, i' faith," answered I, "and I confess my astonishment at finding a tailor of so much taste and skill in Ajaccio. I shall, with my velvet dress, look like *Jean de Paris* alongside of you."

" My toilet, sir, is pure *Humann*, so don't be astonished any more. My brother and I being exactly of the same size, he has for a joke sent me a complete Parisian wardrobe, which you will understand I only use upon great occasions; as for instance, when Monsieur *le Préfet* passes, when Monsieur *le Général*, commander of the 86th department, makes his tour, or, when I receive a guest like you, sir; particularly as this happy event occurs at a time of such solemn ceremony as the one we are now about to celebrate."

There was in this young man a continual tone of irony, controlled by a superior mind, which, although it frequently placed others in an awkward situation, never passed the bounds of decorum.

I contented myself with bowing my

thanks, while he continued occupied in carefully drawing on a pair of straw colored kid gloves, measured for his hand by Boivin, or Rousseau.

Thus, completely dressed, he really looked like an elegant Parisian.

Meanwhile I was finishing my own toilet.

It struck a quarter before ten o'clock.

" Well," said he, " if you wish to see the play, it is high time for us to take our seats, unless you should prefer taking breakfast first, which I think would be much more reasonable."

" I thank you, I never take breakfast before eleven or twelve o'clock, so I have plenty of time for the two operations."

"Come, then."

I took my hat and followed him.

CHAPTER VII.

From the top of the eight steps leading to the door of the armed castle occupied by Signora de Franchi and her son, I could overlook the whole place.

The village wore a very different aspect from what it had presented the day previous; it was crowded with people, composed, however, entirely of women, and children under twelve years of age; not a man appeared in the streets.

On the first step of the church was a man solemnly girded with a tri-colored scarf, it was the Mayor.

Under the portico, another man, dressed in black, was sitting before a table, upon which was laid a paper covered with writing. This was the Public Notary, and the paper was the deed of reconciliation.

I took my stand on one side of the table with the witnesses of Orlandini.

On the other side stood the witnesses of Colonna.

Lucien, as belonging equally to both parties, stood in the centre behind the Notary.

In the choir of the church, the priests were saying mass.

The clock struck ten.

At this moment a shudder ran through the crowd, and all eyes were turned to the two opposite ends of the street, where, from the hill side, appeared Orlandini, while at the same time Colonna entered from the river side. Both of them were accompanied by their partisans. But according to the articles of agreement none of them carried arms. Had it not been for the crabbed expression of their countenances, one would have taken them for peaceable churchwardens following a procession.

The chiefs of the two parties presented a very remarkable physical contrast. Orlandini, as I have already said, was tall, thin, dark complexioned and agile.

Colonna was short, heavy and vigorous; his hair and beard were red, short, and curled.

Both chiefs carried in their hands a branch of olive tree, a symbolical emblem of the peace which they were going to conclude; this was one of the Mayor's poetical inventions.

Colonna also carried by the feet a white hen, destined to serve as damages for the one which ten years before had given rise to the quarrel.

The hen was a living one. This point had been long discussed, and was very near causing the whole affair to be a failure—Colonna considering it a double humiliation to give back a living hen, when his aunt had thrown a dead one into the face of Orlandini's cousin.

However, by means of logical arguments, Lucien had prevailed upon Colonna to give the hen, and by the power of similar demonstrations, had determined Orlandini to accept it.

At the moment when the two enemies made their appearance, the church bells, which had been silent for some time, began to ring violently.

Upon seeing each other, both Colonna and Orlandini made a movement, which left no doubt of their mutual repulsion; nevertheless they continued to advance.

They halted directly in front of the church door, and stood opposite each other, about four steps apart.

If, three days before, these two men had met at a hundred steps' distance, one of them would certainly have fallen on the spot.

During five minutes there reigned, not only in the two parties, but also in the whole crowd, a silence, which, notwithstanding the amicable and reconciling character of the ceremony, had nothing in it of a very peaceful expression.

The Mayor then said in a loud voice.

" Well, Colonna, you know that you have to speak first."

Colonna made a great effort, and pronounced a few words in the Corsican dialect.

It seemed to me that he expressed his regret for having passed ten years in *vendetta* with his good neighbor Orlandini, and he offered him the white hen which he carried as a reparation.

Orlandini waited until the speech of his adversary was fully terminated, and promised in another few Corsican words, not to remember any thing but the solemn reconciliation which was taking place, under the auspices of the Signor Mayor, the arbitration of Signor Lucien,

and the arrangement of the Signor Notary.

They then both became silent again.

" Well, signori," said the Mayor, " it was agreed upon, I believe, that you should shake hands with each other."

By an instinctive movement, the two enemies put their hands behind them.

The Mayor descended the steps upon which he was standing, took Colonna's hand from behind his back, then got hold of Orlandini's hand, and after some efforts, which he tried to hide from the by-standers by smiling, he succeeded in joining their hands.

The Notary took advantage of that moment, rose, and commenced reading the following, while the Mayor still kept the two hands joined, which at first did all they could to disunite, but finally consented to remain together.

" Before us, Guiseppe-Antonio-Sarrola, Notary Royal, at Sullacaro, Province of Sartene ;

" On the square of the village, in front of the church, in presence of the Signor Mayor, the witnesses and the whole population ;

"Between Gaetano-Orso Orlandi, called Orlandini,

"And Marco-Vincenzio Colonna, called Schioppone,

" Has been concluded as follows, viz : From this day, March 9th of the year 1841, the *vendetta* existing between them for the last ten years shall cease.

" From the same day they will live together like good neighbors and companions, as their parents did before this unfortunate occurrence, which has brought disunion between their families and friends.

" In faith of which, they have signed these presents, under the portico of the village church, with Signor Paolo Arbori, Mayor of the Community, Signor Lucien de Franchi, Arbiter, the witnesses of both parties, and ourselves the Notary.

" Sullacaro, this 9th day of March, 1841."

It gave me pleasure to observe, with what excessive prudence the Notary had avoided mentioning a single word about the hen, which placed Colonna in so bad a position before Orlandini.

After the reading of the deed, Colonna's face brightened up, while Orlandini's brow grew darker; he evidently looked at the hen as if he felt the most violent desire of throwing it into Colonnas face; but a glance from Lucien de Franchi prevented the execution of this bad design.

The Mayor saw that there was no time to be lost; he stepped back, still keeping the two hands joined in each other, and not losing sight of the newly reconciled men for a single moment.

Then, in order to prevent a new discussion at the moment of signing, as either of the parties might have considered it a concession to sign first, he took the pen, signed his name, and offered it to Orlandini, thus preventing any hesitation by conferring an honor. Orlandini took the pen, signed, and presented it to Lucien, who, using the same peaceable subterfuge, passed it on in his turn to Colonna, who last of all made his cross.

At this moment solemn music was heard from the church, sounding like the Te Deum sung after a victory.

We then all signed without any distinction of rank or title, just as the nobility of France had, 123 years before, signed the protestation against the *Duc du Maine.*

The two heroes of the day now entered the church, and knelt down on each side of the choir, at the places which had been reserved for them.

I saw that, from this moment only, Lucien became calm. All was over, the reconciliation was sworn, not only before men, but also before God.

The remainder of divine service passed over without any occurrence worth relating.

After the mass was ended, Orlandini and Colonna walked out with the same ceremony. At the door, by the request of the Mayor, they again touched each other's hands. Then each of them, accompanied by their several friends and relations, walked up to his own house, which for the last three years neither of them had entered.

As for Lucien and myself, we returned to Signora de Franchi, where dinner was waiting for us.

It was easy for me to see by the increased attention of which I was the object, that Lucien had read my name when I signed the deed of reconciliation, and that this name was not quite unknown to him.

In the morning I announced to Lucien, my intention of leaving immediately after dinner.

I was anxiously expected at Paris for the rehearsal of " *Un Mariage sous Louis XV,*" and notwithstanding the entreaties of mother and son, firmly adhered to my first decision.

Lucien then asked the permission of writing to his brother, and Madame de Franchi, who with an appearance of classical severity still possessed all the tenderness of a mother's heart, made me promise that I would deliver it to her son with my own hand.

This was certainly no great trouble, as Louis de Franchi, like a true Parisian, lived at No. 7, *Rue du Helder.*

I requested permission to see Lucien's room once more. He took me there himself, and pointing with his hand to all its contents,

" You know, said he, " that if any thing here pleases you, you must take it, for it is yours."

I took down a small poniard which was suspended in a corner sufficiently obscure to convince me that it was not of much value: and as I had seen him throw a glance of admiration on my hunting girdle, and heard him praise its arrangement, I begged him to accept it. He had the good sense to take it, without making me repeat my request.

At this moment Griffo appeared at the door, to inform me that my horse was saddled, and my guide waiting for me.

I had put aside a present which I had reserved for Griffo; it was a kind of hunter's knife, with two pistols attached to it alongside of the blade, the hammers of which were hid in the handle.

I have never seen greater delight exhibited than when I presented it to him.

I went down stairs and found Madame de Franchi waiting to bid me farewell, at the very place where she had welcomed me. I kissed her hand, with a feeling of great admiration for this woman so simple and so dignified.

Lucien accompanied me to the door.

"On any other day," said he, "I should have saddled my horse, and attended you over the mountain, but to-day I dare not leave Sullacaro, for fear that one or the other of our two friends might commit some folly.

"And you do very right," replied I; "as for me, believe me, I am very happy in having witnessed at Corsica such a novel ceremony as the one in which I have taken part."

"Yes, yes, be proud of it, for you have seen that which must have shaken the bones of our ancestors in their graves."

"I understand; with them the war was holy enough, and they would not have needed a notary to draw up an act of reconciliation."

"Or, rather, they would not have consented to a reconciliation at all."

He offered me his hand.

"Do n't you wish me to embrace your brother?" said I.

"Certainly I do, if it will be agreeable to you."

"Well, then, let us embrace each other; I cannot give him what I have not received."

We embraced each other.

"Shall I not see you again?" asked I.

"Yes, if you return to Corsica."

"No, but when you come to Paris?"

"I shall never go there," said Lucien.

"If you ever should, you will find my card on your brother's chimney; do n't forget my name."

"I promise you, that if any event should take me to the continent, I shall make you my first visit."

"Very well, that 's all settled."

He offered me his hand once more, and we parted. He followed me with his eyes, as long as he could see me in the street leading to the river.

The village was tolerably quiet. Only here and there I noticed that kind of agitation which follows great events, and I proceeded, fixing my eyes on each door as I passed, in the expectation of seeing Orlandini come out, who in truth owed me his thanks; but he seemed to have forgotten all about this debt.

And I passed the last house of the village without having seen any thing like him.

I thought he in reality had neglected me, but I must say, that amid the grave occupations with which Orlandini was necessarily engrossed on such a day, I sincerely forgave and excused such forgetfulness. But suddenly, while approaching the forest of Bicchisano, I saw a man come out of the wood, and place himself in the middle of the road. I recognized him immediately to be the very man whom, in my French impatience, and in my habit of Parisian consistency, I had already accused of ingratitude.

I observed that he had found time to put the same dress on again, in which I had first seen him in the ruins of Vincentello; he wore his cartouchière, from which was suspended the indispensable pistol; and he also had his gun with him.

When I was about twenty steps from him, he took off his hat, while at the same time I spurred my horse on, in order not to let him wait.

"Signor," said he, "I did not wish you to leave Sullacaro, without thanking you for the honor you have bestowed on a poor peasant like me by serving him as a witness; and as down there I had not a heart at ease, nor a tongue at liberty, I preferred to wait for you here."

"I am much obliged to you," answered I, "but you should not have disturbed yourself in your occupations for that; I assure you that all the honor has been for me."

"And then, signor," continued the bandit, "how can I help it? No one can, in an instant, give up a habit of three years. The mountain air is strange and mighty; once having inhaled it, you suffocate in any other atmosphere. A little while ago, while in those miserable houses, I thought every moment that the roof would have fallen on my head."

"But," said I, "are you not going now to resume your former mode of life? I understand that you have a house, a field, and a vineyard."

"Yes—I have; but my sister took care of my house, and the *Luquois*

were there to cultivate my field and vineyard. We Corsicans never work."

"What is then your occupation?"

"We superintend the laborers; we walk about with a gun on our shoulders, and go hunting."

"Well, my dear Signor Orlandini," said I, shaking hands with him, "good luck! Remember that my honor, as well as yours, is solemnly pledged for your not shooting in future at any thing else than moufflons, deer, boars, pheasants and partridges, but never at Marco-Vincenzio Colonna, nor at any of his family or friends!"

"Ah! eccellenza," replied he, with an expression of physiognomy which I had never seen before, but on the face of a Norman litigant, "the hen which he returned me was a very poor one!"

And without uttering another word he returned to the thicket, and immediately disappeared.

I continued my road, making some reflections upon this, as a probable reason for a new rupture between the Orlandini and the Colonna.

The same evening I slept at *Albiteccia*. The next day I arrived at Ajaccio. Eight days after, I reached Paris.

CHAPTER VIII.

The very evening I arrived, I went to visit Monsieur Louis de Franchi; he had gone out.

I left my card, with a line informing him that I had arrived direct from Sullacaro, and that I was the bearer of a letter for him from his brother Lucien. I requested him to name his time, adding that I had pledged my word to deliver this letter personally.

In conducting me to the cabinet of his master, where I had to write this note, the servant led me through the dining-room and parlor. I gazed round with a curiosity which every one will easily understand. I recognized the same tastes which I had already noticed at Sullacaro, only they were more refined by Parisian elegance. Monsieur de Franchi appeared to have a delightful bachelor residence.

The following day, while I was dressing, that is to say, about eleven o'clock in the morning, my servant announced Monsieur de Franchi. I gave orders to have him ushered into the *salon*, to offer him the papers, and inform him that in a moment I would be at his service.

Indeed, in five minutes after, I entered the *salon*.

At the noise which I made, Monsieur de Franchi, who, no doubt out of courtesy, was reading one of my *feuilletons*, published at that time in the papers, raised his head.

I remained petrified with his resemblance to his brother.

He rose.

"Monsieur," said he, "I could hardly believe in my good fortune yesterday, while reading the little note which my servant handed me when I came home. I made him repeat the description of your person ten times, in order to ascertain if it corresponded with your portraits. At last, this morning in my double impatience to thank you, and to receive news from my family, I have introduced myself here, without having consulted the hour much; I am therefore afraid I have been too early."

"I beg your pardon," replied I, "for not answering your agreeable compliment at first; but I declare, that looking at you, I have to ask myself if it is to Monsieur Louis or to Monsieur Lucien de Franchi that I have the honor of addressing myself."

"Yes, in truth, the resemblance is great," continued he, smiling, "and when I was at Sullacaro, my brother and myself were the only persons who did not mistake us. However, since I left, he has not abandoned his Corsican habits; you must have seen him constantly in a dress which produces some difference between us."

"Ah! truly," replied I; "but by chance it happened that when I left him he was dressed exactly like you, with the exception only of white pantaloons, which are not yet in season at Paris. So I have not even to separate your resemblance from my remembrance of him on account of the difference in dress of which you speak. But," continued I, taking the letter out of my pocket-book, "I can understand your haste to receive news from your family; therefore take this letter, which I should have left here yesterday, had I not promised Madame De Franchi to deliver it personally."

"And you have left every body in good health?"

"Yes, but in uneasiness."

"About me?"

"About you. But pray read the letter."

"You permit me?"

"How can you ask?"

Monsieur de Franchi unsealed the letter, while I was preparing cigarettes. Meanwhile, I regarded him attentively while he glanced rapidly over the fraternal missive. From time to time he smiled, exclaiming, "This dear Louis! Ah! this good mother! Yes—I understand!"

I had not yet recovered from this strange resemblance; however, as Lucien had told me, I observed a greater delicacy in the complexion of Louis, and a much more correct pronunciation of the French language.

"Well," began I, when he had finished, offering him a cigarette, which he lighted at mine, "you have seen there what I have already told you, that your family are uneasy about you, and I see with pleasure they have been wrong."

"No," said he, with sadness, "not altogether wrong. It is true, I have not been sick, but I have had sorrow; a violent one even, which I confess was augmented by the idea that while I was suffering here, I caused my brother to suffer at home."

"Monsieur Lucien has already told me what you mention now. But really, to make me believe that so extraordinary a thing was true, and not merely a prepossession of his mind, I needed nothing less than the proof I have received this moment. So you are yourself convinced that the uneasiness your brother felt in Corsica, was in consequence of your state of suffering here?"

"Yes, sir, perfectly."

"Then, as your answer in the affirmative has had the effect of doubly interesting me in all that happens to you, permit me to ask, not out of curiosity, but from the interest I feel in you, if the grief of which you spoke just now has not passed away, and if you are not in the way to receive consolation?"

"Alas! You know, sir, that the most violent grief becomes deadened by time, and if no fatality occurs to irritate the wound of my heart, well! then it may bleed a little longer, and finally become seared. Meanwhile, receive again all my thanks, and grant me from time to time the permission to call upon you, and talk about Sullacaro."

"With the greatest pleasure," replied I; "but why do we not this very moment continue a conversation which is as agreeable to me as it is to yourself? Hold! there comes my servant to inform me that breakfast is ready; do me the favor of eating a cutlet with me, and then we can talk at our ease."

"Impossible! to my deep regret. I received yesterday a letter from the Lord Chancellor, who has invited me to pass to-day at noon at the Ministry of Justice; and you well know that I, a poor little sprig of a lawyer, cannot let such a great personage wait."

"Ah! but it is probably about the affair between the Orlandini and the Colonna that he sends for you."

"I presume so; and as my brother informs me that the quarrel is terminated—"

"Before the Notary I can give you very certain news on the subject; I have signed the contract as one of Orlandini's witnesses."

"Yes; my brother says something about that."

"But see here," continued he, drawing out his watch, "it is only a few minutes before noon; I must go and inform the Lord Chancellor that my brother has fulfilled my word."

"Oh! religiously!—I'll warrant you."

"That dear Lucien! I knew that, notwithstanding it did not agree with his views, he would do it."

"Yes; and you must give him credit for it—for I assure you it has cost him dear."

"We will speak of that again, for, believe me, it affords me the greatest happiness to behold again, in the mind's eye at least, my mother, my brother, my country! So, if you'll tell me your hour—"

"That is rather difficult just now. During the first few days after my return, I am going to be something of a vagabond. But tell me where I can find you?"

"Listen," said he; "to-morrow is Mid-Lent, is it not?"

"To-morrow?"

"Yes."

"Well?"

"Do you go to the ball of the Opera?"

"Yes, and no. Yes, if you ask me that to give me a rendezvous there; no—if I have no other interest to go there."

"I, for my part, shall have to go. I am obliged to go there."

"Ah! ha!" said I, with a smile; "I see, as you said awhile ago, that time blunts the most poignant griefs, and I have no doubt that the wound of your heart will soon become healed."

"You are mistaken, for I am probably going to seek there new torments."

"Don't go, then."

"Who in this world does what he wishes to do? I am carried away in spite of myself; I go where fate impels me. It would be better not to go; I know it—but, nevertheless, I shall go!"

"Then, till to-morrow!—at the Opera!"

"Just so."

"At what hour?"

"At half-past twelve—if you will."

"And where?"

"In the green-room, at one o'clock. I have a rendezvous before the *pendule!*"

"Agreed!"

We shook hands, and he went rapidly out. Soon after it struck twelve.

As for me, I occupied my whole afternoon and the following day with all those visits indispensable in a man who has made a journey of eighteen months.

At half-past twelve o'clock, on the appointed day, I was at the rendezvous.

Louis kept me waiting some time. He had followed in the corridor a mask, which he thought he recognized; but the mask had lost itself in the crowd, and he could not meet with it again.

I began to speak of Corsica, but Louis was too much disturbed to follow so grave a subject of conversation. His eyes were constantly fixed on the *pendule*, and suddenly he left me, exclaiming—

"Ah! there is my bouquet of *violets!*"

And he plunged into the crowd, in order to approach a female who held an enormous bunch of violets in her hand.

As, fortunately for the promenaders, there was in the green-room plenty of bouquets, I was soon accosted myself by a bunch of *camelias*, which was kind enough to compliment me on my happy return to Paris.

The bunch of camelias was soon followed by a bunch of large roses.

At last I was just at my fifth bunch, when I met Dujarrier.

"Ah! is that you, *mon cher?*" said he, "welcome! You arrive in marvelous good time. We take supper this evening at my house, with this one, and that one,"—he named to me three or four of our mutual friends—"and we depend on you."

"A thousand thanks, *mon cher*," replied I; "notwithstanding my great desire to accept your invitation, I cannot do it, as I have some one with me."

"But it seems to me a matter of course that every one has a right to bring his partner along. It is perfectly well understood that there will be on the table six water bottles, for the purpose of keeping the bouquets fresh."

"Ah! my dear friend, you are mistaken. I have no bunch of flowers for your decanters; I am with a male friend."

"Well, but you know the proverb, 'the friend of our friends—'"

"He is a young man whom you do not know."

"Well, we shall become acquainted."

"I shall propose him this good fortune."

"Yes; and if he refuses, bring him by force."

"I'll do what I can—I promise you. And what is your supper hour?"

"Three o'clock; but as it will last till six, you will have some grace."

"Very well."

A bunch of *myosotis*, who had probably overheard the last part of our conversation, suddenly took hold of D——'s arm, and disappeared with him.

A few minutes after, I met Louis again, who had in all probability finished with his bouquet of *violets*.

As my domino was of rather a slender capacity, I sent it to tease one of my friends, and took Louis' arm.

"Well," began I, "did you learn what you wanted to know?"

"Mon Dieu! yes! you know that generally at a masquerade ball we are often told things which we had rather not know?"

"My poor friend," said I; "pardon me for giving you that name, but it seems to me as if I had known you ever since I first saw your brother. Let us see; you feel unhappy, do you? What is the matter?"

"Nothing worth relating."

I saw that he wished to keep his secret, and I was silent.

We walked round two or three times in silence; I, rather indifferent, for I expected nobody; he, all the time on the look-out, and examining every domino which passed within reach of our sight.

"Look here," said I; "do you know what you ought to do?"

He trembled like a man who is forcibly diverted from his pain.

"Me? No! What did you say? Pardon me!"

"I am going to propose a diversion to you, which I think you need."

"What is it?"

"Come and take supper with me at the house of a friend of mine."

"Oh, no! I am afraid I should be too dull a companion."

"Bah! you'll hear some *folies*, and that will cheer you up."

"Besides, I am not invited."

"That's where you are mistaken; you are invited."

"That is certainly very kind in your Amphytrion, but, on my honor, I don't feel worthy." . . . .

At this moment we came across Dujarrier; he seemed very much engrossed with his bouquet of *myosotis*. Nevertheless he noticed me.

"Well," said he, "it is all settled, is it not?"

"Till three o'clock."

"Less agreed than ever, *mon cher ami*, I can't be of your company."

"Go to the devil then."

And he continued his walk.

"Who is that gentleman?" asked Louis, evidently only to say something.

"Why, that's Dujarrier, one of our friends, a fellow of great mind, although he is editor of one of our first papers."

"Monsieur Dujarrier!" exclaimed Louis; "Monsieur Dujarrier! You are acquainted with him?"

"Certainly I am; for two or three years past I have been in relations of interest, and especially of friendship with him."

"It is with him you intend taking supper to-night?"

"Exactly?"

"Then it was to his house that you offered to take me?"

"Yes."

"Ah! that's quite another thing; I accept your invitation then. Yes, I accept it with great pleasure."

"Very well. I have not gained your consent without some difficulty."

"Perhaps I ought not to go there," replied Louis, smiling sadly; "but you know what I told you the day before yesterday; we go not where we ought to go, but where fate drives us; and the proof of this is that I would have done better not to have come here this evening."

At this moment we crossed Dujarrier again.

"My dear friend," said I, "I have changed my mind."

"And you are of our party to-night?"

"Yes."

"Bravo! But I have to tell you of another circumstance."

"What is it?"

"Whoever takes supper with us to-night, must do so again the day after to-morrow."

"By virtue of what law?"

"Merely on account of a bet made with Château-Renaud."

I felt Louis tremble with excessive agitation, his arm being within mine. I turned round, but although his face was rather paler than before, his features remained unmoved.

"And pray what is the object of this bet?" continued I, speaking to Dujarrier.

"Oh! that would take too long to tell you here. Besides, there is a person here, interested in this bet, who could make him lose, if she overheard it spoken of."

"Excellent! Till three o'clock then?"

"Till three o'clock."

We separated once more. In passing before the *pendule* I gave a glance at the dial; it was thirty-five minutes past two.

"Are you acquainted with Monsieur de Château-Renaud?" asked Louis in a voice the emotion of which he vainly tried to dissimulate.

"By sight only; I have sometimes met with him in society."

"He is then not one of your friends?"

"He is not even an acquaintance of mine."

"Ah! so much the better," said Louis.

"Why so?"

"Oh! nothing."

"But you, do you know him?"

"Indirectly, I do."

Notwithstanding the evasive character of his answer, I could easily perceive that there existed between Monsieur de Franchi and Monsieur de Château Renaud, one of those mysterious relations, the conductor of which is a woman. An instinctive feeling told me it would be better for my companion that we should both return home.

"Now see here, Mons. de Franchi," began I, "will you believe in my advice?"

"What is it? speak!"

"Let us not go to D's to supper."

"But why not? does he not expect

us? and have you not told him already that you would bring me along?"

"Certainly I have, but that is not my reason."

"What is it, then?"

"Because I merely think it would be better for us not to go there."

"But, finally, you have a reason for thus changing your mind; awhile ago you insisted upon taking me there almost in spite of myself."

"We should only meet Monsieur de Château-Renaud."

"So much the better. He is said to be very agreeable, and I would be delighted to make a more intimate acquaintance with him."

"Well then, be it so," replied I. "We will go then because you wish it."

We went down stairs to get our *paletots*. Monsieur Dujarrier lived only a few doors from the opera house. It was delightful weather, and as I thought the fresh air would serve to calm the mind of my companion a little, I proposed taking a short walk, to which he assented.

We found in the *salon* several of my friends, loungers of the green-room of the opera, tenants of that infernal box of *B.—L.—V.—A A*. Besides, as I had suspected, two or three dominos unmasked, keeping their bouquets of flowers in their hands, waiting for the moment of placing them in the decanters.

I introduced Louis de Franchi to one and another; he was of course politely received by all of them.

In about ten minutes after Dujarrier arrived, in his turn, introducing the bouquet of *myosotis*, who took her mask off with an *abandon* and ease, which indicated first the beautiful woman, and then one accustomed to this kind of society.

I presented M. de Franchi to Dujarrier.

"Now," said one of the guests, M. de B., "if the introductions are all over, I propose that we sit down to supper."

"All the introductions are made, but all the guests have not yet arrived," said Dujarrier.

"And who is to come yet?"

"Château-Renaud has not arrived yet."

"Ah! that's true, is there not a bet pending?" asked V.

"Yes, the bet is a supper for twelve persons, that he will not bring a certain lady, whom he has pledged himself to bring here."

"And, pray, who is this lady," asked the bouquet of *myosotis*, "who is so shy as to be the object of such bets?"

I looked at de Franchi; he was apparently calm, but as pale as death.

"Upon my soul," said Dujarrier, "I don't think it would be a great indiscretion to give the name of the mask, especially as in all probability you don't know her. It is Madame ——"

Louis put his hand on D's arm.

"Sir," said he to him, "for the sake of our new acquaintance, grant me one favor."

"What is it?"

"Do not name the person who is coming with Mons. Château-Renaud; you know that she is a married lady."

"Yes, but her husband is at Smyrna, in the Indies, at Mexico, or I don't know where; and you know that when a husband is so far away it is just as good as if he were no longer in existence."

"Her husband will be back in a few days. I know him: he is an honorable man, and I wish, if possible, to save him the grief of learning on his return, that his wife has committed an indiscretion of this kind."

"In that case, excuse me, sir," said D., I was ignorant of your acquaintance with this lady; I was not even aware that she was married. But as you know her and know her husband too—"

"I know him."

"We shall act with the greatest discretion. Ladies and gentlemen, M. Château-Renaud may, or may not come; he may come alone, or accompanied by a lady—he may lose, or not lose his bet; in all cases, I request you to keep this adventure secret."

They all with one voice promised, as he requested; probably not from a very deep sentiment of social propriety, but because every body was very hungry, and consequently desirous of sitting down to supper."

"Thank you, sir," said de Franchi to Dujarrier, offering him his hand; "I assure you that you have acted like a gallant man."

We passed out into the *salle à manger*, and each one took his seat. Two places remained vacant; those of Château-Renaud and the lady who was to accompany him.

The servant was about taking these two covers away—

"No," said the master of the house, "let them remain, "Mons. Château-Renaud has time till four o'clock. At that hour you may remove them, he will have lost his bet."

I did not lose sight of M. de Franchi. I saw him glancing at the *pendule*, it wanted twenty minutes to four.

"Is your time right?" asked Louis carelessly.

"That's not my business," answered Dujarrier, laughing, "Château-Renaud must look to that! I have regulated my *pendule* after his watch, so that he cannot complain of having been mistaken in the time."

"Ah! gentlemen," said the bouquet of *myosotis*, "*pour Dieu*, since it is forbidden, do not let us speak any more of Château-Renaud and his fair *inconnue*, for we are about falling into symbols, allegories and enigmas, which with your permission are horribly *ennuyeux*."

"You are right, Est—" replied V., "there are many ladies of whom we can speak, and who do n't wish any thing better than to be spoken of."

"To their health!" said Dujarrier.

The glasses were filling with iced Champagne. Each guest had his bottle at hand.

I noticed that Louis only touched his glass slightly with his lips.

"But drink," said I to him, "you see well enough that he will not come."

"It is yet a quarter to four. At four o'clock, no matter how much behindhand I may be, I promise you I will go ahead of the one who is most in advance."

"All right then."

While we exchanged these few words in a low tone of voice, the conversation became general and noisy. From time to time Dujarrier and Louis both looked at the *pendule*, which continued pursuing its imperturbable march, perfectly insensible of the impatience of the two persons who were anxiously watching its hands.

At five minutes to four, I looked at Louis. "Your health," said I.

He took his glass, smiling, and brought it up to his lips.

He had emptied just about one half of it, when the bell rung.

I had thought he could not become any paler. I was mistaken.

"That's he," said Louis.

"We shall soon see that."

The ringing of the bell had attracted the attention of the whole company; and the most profound silence immediately followed the noisy conversation which was running round and crossing the whole table. Something like a discussion was heard in the antichamber.

Dujarrier rose, and opened the door.

"I have recognized her voice," said Louis, seizing my wrist and pressing it with great force.

"Come, come,—courage now, be a man," answered I; "it is evident that if she comes to take supper at the house of a man and with people with all of whom she is entirely unacquainted, she is a woman who does not deserve the love of an honorable man."

"But pray, madame," said D., in the antichamber, "walk in, if you please, I assure you that we are altogether among friends."

"Come in, my dear Emily," said Monsieur Château-Renaud ; "you shall not take your mask off, if you do n't choose to do so."

"The wretch!" murmured Louis.

At this moment the lady entered, drawn rather than led by Château-Renaud, and Dujarrier, who fancied himself obliged to perform this office as master of the house.

"Three minutes to four," said Château-Renaud to D., in a low voice.

"Very well, mon cher, you have won."

"Not yet, sir," said the unknown lady, speaking to Château-Renaud, and raising herself to her full height. "I understand, now, why you persisted; you have made a bet to bring me here to supper, have you not?"

Château-Renaud remained silent. She then addressed herself to D.

"As this man will not reply, will you please to answer me, sir? Has not Monsieur Château-Renaud made a bet to bring me here to take supper with you?"

"I cannot deny, madame, that Monsieur Château-Renaud has flattered me with that hope."

"Well, Monsieur Château-Renaud has lost then, for I was not aware of the place to which he was conducting me, and thought I was going to take supper with a lady, one of my friends. Now, as I did not come here willingly, it seems to me that Monsieur de Château-Renaud ought to lose the benefit of his bet."

"But now that you are here, my dear Emily, replied Monsieur de Château-Renaud, you 'll stay, wont you? You see we have good company in these gentlemen, and you will have merry companions in these ladies."

"Now that I am here," said the inconnue, "I thank the gentleman who seems to be the master of the house for the kind reception he has been pleased to give me; but, as unfortunately I cannot accept this polite invitation, I shall request M. Louis de Franchi to give me his arm and see me home."

Louis de Franchi sprung up, and in an instant placed himself between M. de Château-Renaud and the inconnue.

"I wish you to observe, madame," said the latter, clenching his teeth with anger, "that it is I who brought you here; consequently, it is my duty to see you home."

"Gentlemen," said the inconnue, "you are five here, and I put myself under the guard of your honor. You will, I hope, prevent Mons. de Château-Renaud from using any violence upon me."

Château-Renaud made a movement, we all rose at once.

" Very well, madame," said he, " you are at liberty to act as you please. I know whom I shall have to thank for this."

"If it is me you mean, sir," said Louis de Franchi, with an air of haughtiness impossible to describe, " you will find me all day to-morrow at No. 7, Rue du Helder."

"Very well, sir, perhaps I shall not have the honor of calling on you in person, but I hope you will be kind enough to receive two of my friends in my place."

" There was nothing else wanting in you, sir," said Louis de Franchi, shrugging his shoulders, " but to give such a rendezvous before a lady. Come, madame," continued he, taking the arm of the *incônnue*, " and believe me, I thank you sincerely for the honor you do me."

They both went out, amid a profound silence.

" Well, what now, gentlemen?" began Château-Renaud, as soon as the door closed; " I have lost my bet, that's all. The day after to-morrow evening we —all who are here, will meet at the Frères-Provençaux."

He sat down in one of the empty seats, and reached his glass over to Dujarrier, who filled it up to the brim.

Meanwhile, in spite of the noisy gaiety of M. de Château-Renaud, the remainder of the supper passed off rather dull.

The following morning, or rather the same day, I found myself at ten o'clock in the morning, at the door of Louis de Franchi's residence.

As I ascended the steps, I met two gentlemen coming down. One of them was evidently a man of the world. The other one, decorated with the Legion-d'Honneur, appeared, notwithstanding his citizen's dress, to be a military man. I had no doubt that these gentlemen came from Monsieur de Franchi; I followed them with my eyes to the foot of the stairs, and then continued my way and rung the bell.

The servant opened the door. His master was in his cabinet.

When he entered to announce me, Louis, who was occupied in writing a note, turned his head.

" Ah! is that you!" said he, crushing the note in his hand and throwing it into the fire, " this note was addressed to you, and I was just going to send it. Very well,—Joseph, I am not at home to any body this morning."

The servant left the room.

" Did you not meet two gentlemen on the staircase?" continued Louis, drawing forward an arm-chair.

" Yes, one of them was decorated."

" Exactly so."

" I suspected they had been to visit you."

" You guessed right."

" Did they come in the name of M. de Château-Renaud?"

" They are his seconds."

" Ah Diable! he has taken the matter rigorously, it appears."

" He could not do otherwise, you'll acknowledge that," said Louis.

" And they came—"

" To request me to send two of my friends to talk with them about the matter; I then thought of you."

" I am much flattered with your remembrance of me, but I cannot go alone to see them."

" I have sent for one of my friends, the Baron Giordano-Martelli, to take breakfast with us. He will be here at eleven o'clock. We will then breakfast together, and at noon, you will have the kindness to call upon these gentlemen, who have promised to stay at home till three o'clock. Here are their names and residences."

Louis handed me two cards.

One, was that of the Baron Réné de Châteaugrand, the other, of M. Adrien de Boissy. The first lived No 12, Rue de la Paix; the second, who, as I had suspected, belonged to the army, was a lieutenant in the regiment of the *Chasseurs d' Afrique*, and lived at 29, Rue de Lille.

I turned the cards over and over in my hands.

" Well, what embarrasses you ?" asked Louis.

" I would like you to tell me, quite candidly, if you consider this affair as serious. You know that our conduct must be regulated accordingly."

" How is that! as very serious! certainly. Besides, you have heard it. I have placed myself at the disposal of Monsieur de Chàteau-Renaud, and he has sent me his seconds; I have therefore nothing else to do, but to let things take their course."

" Yes, certainly, but—"

" Go on," said Louis, smiling.

" But at least we ought to know what you are going to fight about. One cannot see two people cutting each other's throats, without at least wishing to learn the motive of the combat. You know very well that the position of the seconds is more important than that of the fighter."

" Well, then, I will tell you, in two words, the cause of this quarrel. On my arrival at Paris, one of my friends, the captain of a frigate, introduced me to his wife. She was young and handsome. The sight of her made so deep an impression upon me, that fearing I might fall in love with her, I seldom took advantage of the permission I had

received, of coming to the house at any hour. My friend complained of my indifference, and I then openly told him the truth; that is to say, that his wife was too charming in every respect, for me to run the risk of seeing her too frequently. He smiled, gave me his hand and invited me to dinner the same day."

" My dear Louis," said he, at the dessert, " I leave in three weeks for Mexico; perhaps I shall be gone three months, perhaps six months, or even more. We sailors know sometimes the hour of parting, but never the time of our return. In my absence I commend my Emily to your care. And you, Emily, I request you to treat Louis de Franchi as a brother."

The young lady answered, by offering me her hand.

" I was surprised, I did not know what to say, and I must certainly have appeared very insipid to my future sister."

" Three months after, in fact, my friend departed. During these three months, he had prevailed upon me to take dinner with them without ceremony, at least once a week."

" Emily remained with her mother. It is not necessary to tell you, that the confidence of her husband had made her sacred to me, and that although loving her more than it was necessary for a brother, I never looked upon her but as a sister.

" Six months passed away. Emily resided with her mother, and her husband, upon leaving, had requested her to continue to receive company. My poor friend was very much afraid of the reputation of being jealous.

" In fact he adored Emily and had the fullest confidence in her.

" So Emily continued to see company.

However, she only received intimate acquaintances, and the presence of her mother prevented the most malicious tongues from blaming her. But no one ever dared to breathe a single word which could have sullied her reputation.

"Some three months since, Monsieur de Château-Renaud got introduced to her. You believe in presentiments, do you? At sight of him, I trembled. He did not speak to me. He was, what a man of the world is, in a *salon*, but notwithstanding, when he left, I already hated him. Why, I did not know myself.

"Or, rather, I had perceived that he felt the same impression which had been made upon me, when I saw Emily for the first time.

"As for her, it appeared to me that Emily had received him with more than usual coquetry.

"No doubt this was a mistake; but I have told you that in the depths of my heart I had never ceased loving Emily, and I was jealous.

"So, on the next reception day, I did not lose sight of Monsieur de Château-Renaud. Perhaps he noticed my pertinacity in following him with my eyes; and it seemed to me, that while talking in a low tone to Emily, he tried to make me appear ridiculous.

"If I had only attended to the voice of my heart, I should have sought a quarrel with him that very evening, and under any pretext would have fought a duel with him. But I controlled myself, considering that such conduct would be absurd.

"But how could I help it? every Friday after this was a torment to me. Mons. de Château-Renaud being altogether a man of the world, a fashionable, a lion, I was forced to acknowledge his superiority over me, in many respects; but I thought that Emily placed him still higher than he deserved.

"Soon after, it appeared that I was not the only person who noticed this preference of Emily for Monsieur de Château-Renaud; a preference which increased so rapidly and so visibly, that one day Giordano, who like me visited her house, spoke to me about it.

"From that time my decision was taken. I determined to speak to Emily on the subject, as I was convinced there was only a thoughtlessness on her part, which would make it merely necessary for me to open her eyes to her own conduct, to change all which so far had been calculated to fix upon her the charge of levity.

"But, to my great surprise, Emily took my observations as a joke, pretending that I was foolish, and that all who thought as I did, were as silly as myself.

"I insisted.

"Emily then answered that she could not rely upon me in a matter of this kind, and that a lover was necessarily a partial judge.

"I remained amazed; her husband had told her all.

"From this time, regarded in the light of a disappointed and jealous lover, my position became odious and nearly ridiculous. I ceased visiting Emily.

"But I still continued to receive news from her, and was not the less unhappy for that, for the assiduities of Château-Renaud to Emily began to be generally noticed, and openly spoken of.

"I resolved to write to her. I did so in the most careful and studied manner of which I was capable, beseeching her in the name of her compromised honor, in the name of her absent husband, who was full of confidence in her, to keep a strict watch over all her actions. She did not answer me.

"How could she help it? Love is independent of the will : the poor creature loved, and because she loved she was blind, or, rather, was determined to be so.

"Some time after this I heard it openly said that Emily was the mistress of Château-Renaud.

"What I then suffered is impossible for me to describe. It was at this period that my poor brother felt, by a peculiar sympathy, the pain I endured.

"Meanwhile, some ten or twelve days elapsed, during which time you arrived.

"The very day upon which you first called at my house, I had received an anonymous letter. It was from a lady, who gave me a rendezvous at the *Bal de l'Opéra*. She told me that she had certain information to communicate concerning a friend of mine, a lady, but would content herself for the present by telling me her first name.

"That name was Emily.

"I was to recognize her by a bouquet of violets.

"I told you then that I ought not to have gone to the ball; but I now repeat to you that I was impelled by fate!

"I went. I found my domino at the time and place designated. She confirmed all that I had already heard ; that is, that Château-Renaud was Emily's lover ; and as I doubted, or affected to doubt it, she told me as a proof of its truth, that M. de Château-Renaud had made a bet that he would bring his new mistress to Dujarrier's to supper.

"Fate had ordained that you should be acquainted with M. D——, that you were invited to that supper, that you had permission to bring a friend along, that you should have solicited me to accompany you there, and, lastly, that I should go.

"You know the rest.

"Now, what else can I do than to wait and accept the propositions which are going to be made to me ?"

As there was no objection possible to this, I merely bowed my head.

"But," replied I, after a moment, with a faltering of fear, "I believe I recollect—I hope I am mistaken—that your brother told me you had never touched either a pistol or a sword ?"

"That's true."

"But then you are at the mercy of your adversary ?"

"How can I help it? God will watch over it!"

At this moment the servant announced the Baron Giordano-Martelli.

He was, like Louis de Franchi, a young Corsican of the province of Sartene, and served in the 17th regiment. Two or three actions had procured him the rank of captain, at the age of twenty-three years. He was of course in citizen's dress.

"Well," said he, to Louis, after having saluted me, "the matter has now arrived at the point where it must unavoidably have come ; and after what you have written me, I have no doubt that you will receive a visit during the day from the seconds of Monsieur de Château-Renaud."

"I have had it already," said Louis.

"Those gentlemen have left their names and residences ?"

"Here are their cards."

"Well! Your valet has told me that breakfast is ready ; so let us sit down, and after that we will return the visit of these gentlemen."

We passed into the dining room, and the circumstance which had brought us together was not spoken of again.

It was then that Louis questioned me about my journey to Corsica, and here only that I found an opportunity of relating to him what the reader already knows.

In this hour, while the young man's mind was calmed by the idea of fighting with M. de Châteu-Renaud the following day, all the feelings of home and country came back upon his heart. He made me repeat twenty times what his mother and brother had told me to tell him. He was particularly affected —knowing the true Corsican manners of Lucien—by the care which he had taken in pacifying the quarrel of the Orlandini and Colonna.

It struck twelve o'clock.

"I believe—without hurrying you, my friends—that it is time to return the visit of these gentlemen. Waiting longer might lead them to accuse us of neglect."

"Oh! make yourself easy on that point," said I, "they left here only two hours ago, and they must allow you the necessary time to send for us."

"Never mind," said the Baron Giordano, "Louis is right."

"Now," said I to Louis, "it is necessary for us to know which you prefer, sword or pistol?"

"Oh! sir—I have already told you that it is entirely indifferent to me, as I am as unfamiliar with one as the other. Besides, Mons. de Château-Renaud will spare me the embarrassment of the choice. He will, no doubt, consider himself as the offended party, and as such has the right of choosing what weapon he likes best."

"But, notwithstanding, the offence is a matter of discussion. You have done nothing else than to offer the arm which was asked for."

"Listen to me," said Louis; "every discussion, in my opinion, would look like a desire to make an arrangement.

I am naturally very peaceable, you know it; I am far from being a duelist, for this is my first affair; but just for these various reasons I wish to play gallantly."

"Ah! that's very easy for you to say, mon cher; you only run the risk of your life; while you leave to us the responsibility of answering to your whole family the consequences of what may happen."

"Oh! as for that, don't be uneasy! I know my mother and brother. They will merely ask you, 'did Louis act like a gallant man?' And when you tell them, 'Yes!' they will answer, 'That is well!'"

"But, finally, tell us what weapons you prefer."

"Well, if the pistol is proposed, accept it immediately."

"That was my opinion, also," said the Baron.

"Then go for the pistol," replied I, "as it is your opinion, both of you. But the pistol is a villainous weapon."

"Have I time, between this and to-morrow, to learn to fight with a sword?"

"No. But with a good lesson from *Grisier*, you could, perhaps, learn to defend yourself."

Louis smiled.

"Believe me," said he, "all that will happen to me to-morrow morning is already written in the book of fate, and whatever you or I may do cannot change any thing in it."

After this, we shook hands with him, and went out.

Our first visit was, of course, to the second of our adversary who lived nearest to us. We therefore called upon Mons. Réné de Châteaugrand, who lived, as already mentioned, at No. 12, *Rue de la Paix*.

Admittance was denied to all persons

except those who should introduce themselves as coming from Monsieur Louis de Franchi. We signified our mission, presented our cards, and were admitted without further delay.

We found in M. Châteaugrand a man of the world, perfectly elegant. He would not permit us to go to the trouble of calling upon Monsieur de Boissy, but informed us that it had been agreed between them, that whoever should be called upon first by us, should send for the other; and both of them were to hold themselves in readiness to come at a moment's warning. Monsieur de Châteaugrand therefore sent his servant immediately to inform Monsieur de Boissy that we were in waiting at his residence.

During this time there was not for a moment any mention made of the business which had brought us here. We spoke of stakes, hunting, and the opera.

We had been waiting about ten minutes, when Mons. de Boissy arrived.

The two gentlemen did not even pretend to have a choice in the weapons. Sword and pistol were equally familiar to Mons. de Château-Renaud, who left it entirely to the preference of Mons. Louis de Franchi, or to the decision of hazard.

A louisd'or was then thrown in the air, head for the sword, tail for the pistol. The louis fell with the tail up.

It was finally concluded that the duel should take place on the following morning, at nine o'clock, at the *Bois de Vincennes;* that the adversaries were to be placed at twenty steps' distance from each other, that one of the seconds should clap his hands three times as a signal, and that at the third clap they would both fire.

We took this answer to Monsieur de Franchi.

The same evening, after I had returned home, I found the cards of Mons. Châteaugrand and Mons. de Boissy.

CHAPTER IX.

I had been to see Monsieur Louis de Franchi that evening at eight o'clock, to ask him if he had any orders or instructions to give me; but he requested me to wait until the following morning, adding with a strange air—

"Night brings counsel."

Accordingly, on the following morning, instead of calling for him at eight o'clock, which would have left us plenty of time to be at the rendezvous at nine, I was at de Franchi's residence at half-past seven.

He was in his cabinet, writing.

At the noise which I made in opening the door, he turned round. He was very pale.

"Excuse me," he said; "I am just finishing a letter to my mother. Sit down and take a paper, if to-day's papers have come yet. There's *la Presse* for instance—it contains a charming *feuilleton* of Mons. Méry.

I took the paper which he designated, observing with astonishment the contrast between the almost livid paleness of the young man, and his voice, so sweet, grave, and calm.

I tried to read; but I merely followed the words with my eyes, without their presenting any distinct idea to my mind.

In a few minutes he rang the bell for his valet.

"I have finished," said he.

Then speaking to his servant—

"Joseph," continued he, "I am not at home for any body, not even for Giordano. If he should come, invite him into the *salon;* I wish to be alone with this gentleman for a few minutes, without any interruption whatever.

The servant went out and shut the door.

"Well, now, my dear Alexander," began he to me, "Giordano is a Corsican, and has Corsican ideas. I cannot, therefore, confide to him all my wishes. I shall ask him to keep the secret, that is all. As for you, you must promise me to fulfill my instructions to the very letter!"

"Certainly; is that not the duty of a second?"

"Yes; but yours is so much more important, as, by fulfilling it, you will perhaps spare my family a second misfortune."

"A second misfortune?" exclaimed I, in astonishment.

"Hold!" said he, "read this letter I have written to my mother."

I took the letter from de Franchi's hand, and read in increasing amazement:

"MY GOOD MOTHER:

"If I did not know you to be both strong as a Spartan and submissive as a Christian woman, I should employ all possible means to prepare you for the dreadful event which is about to overwhelm you. When you receive this letter, you will have but one son!

"Lucien, my excellent brother, love my mother for both of us.

"The day before yesterday I was attacked with a cerebral fever, and paid but little attention to the first symptoms. The doctor has been called in too late. My dear mother, there is no hope left for me. Nothing less than a miracle could save me, and what right have I to expect that God would work such a wonder for me?

"I write to you in a lucid interval."

"If I die, this letter will be put in the postoffice a quarter of an hour after my death. For, in the egotism of my love for you, I wish you to know that

I have died, regretting nothing in the whole world, but your tenderness and my brother's love.

"Farewell, my mother! Do not weep! It was my soul that loved you, and not my body; and wherever my spirit may go, it will never cease to love you!

"Farewell, Lucien! Never leave our mother! and remember that she has none left but you!

"Your son and brother,
    "LOUIS DE FRANCHI."

After reading these last words, I looked up to him who had written them.

"Well," said I, "what is the meaning of all this?"

"Do n't you understand?"

"No."

"I shall be killed at ten minutes after nine!"

"You will be killed?"

"Yes."

"But you are foolish; why do you indulge in such an idea?"

"I am not foolish; nor do I indulge in any weakness, my dear friend. I have been informed, that 's all."

"Informed! and by whom?"

"Has not my brother told you," said Louis, with a smile, "that the males in our family enjoy a peculiar privilege?"

"He has," replied I, trembling in spite of myself; "he spoke of visions."

"Exactly! Well, my father appeared to me last night; that is the reason you have found mé so pale. The sight of the dead makes the living pale."

I looked at him with an astonishment which was not free from terror.

"You have seen your father last night, you say?"

"Yes."

"And he has spoken to you?"

"He announced my death to me!"

"That was some terrific dream?"

" It was a terrific reality."

" You slept ?"

" I was awake. Do n't you believe that a father can appear to his son ?"

" I bowed my head; for, in the depths of my heart, I believed in such a possibility.

" How did it happen?" asked I again.

" In the most simple and natural manner. I was reading while waiting for my father, for I knew, if I was in any danger, that he would appear to me. At midnight my lamp, without any apparent cause, became dim, the door opened slowly, and my father appeared."

" But how ?"

" Just as he did while living, and dressed in the coat he usually wore ; only, he was very pale and his eyes were without life."

" Oh God !"

" He then slowly approached my bed. I raised myself upon my elbow.

" You are welcome, father," said I.

" He came nearer, looked fixedly at me, and it seemed to me that his lifeless eye animated itself by the force of paternal affection."

" Continue,—this is terrible !"

" Then his lips moved, and strange to say, although his words did not produce any sound, I felt them resounding all through me, distinct and vibrating like an echo."

" And what did he say to you ?"

" Think of God ! my son."

" I am then going to be killed in this duel ? asked I.

" I saw two tears from those lifeless eyes, roll down the pale face of the spectre.

" And at what hour ? continued I.

" He pointed with his finger to the *pendule.* I followed the direction he indicated. The clock showed ten minutes past nine.

" Very well ! my father, replied I, then God's will be done ! It is true I must leave my mother, but I come to rejoin you.

" A feeble smile passed over his pale lips, and making me a farewell sign, he left me. The door opened of itself before him, he disappeared, and the door closed."

This recital was made in such a simple and natural manner, that it was evident to me the scene he had described must actually have taken place, or that, in the pre-occupation of his mind, he had been the sport of an illusion, which, having been taken for a reality, was equally as terrible in its consequences.

I wiped off the sweat, which was running down from my forehead.

" Now," continued Louis, " you know my brother, do you not ?"

" Yes."

" What do you think he would do if he should learn that I have been killed in a duel ?"

" He will that very instant leave Sullacaro, to come here and fight with him who has caused your death."

" Exactly ! and if he is killed in his turn, my mother will be three times a widow. A widow for her husband—a widow for her two sons."

" Oh ! I understand—that is horrible !"

" Well ! it must be avoided ! for that purpose I have written this letter to my mother. Believing that I have died in a brain fever, my brother will not seek revenge upon any body, and my mother will be more easily consoled if she thinks I have been stricken by the will of God, than if she knew I had been destroyed by the hand of man. Unless—"

"Unless?" repeated I.

"Oh, no!" said Louis, " I hope that that will not be the case."

I saw that he answered his own fears, and did not insist any further.

At this moment, the door opened.

"My dear de Franchi," said Baron de Giordano, "I have respected your orders as long as it was possible ; but it is eight o'clock, the rendezvous is at nine, and we have a league and a half to travel. We must start."

"I am ready, my dear friend," said Louis. "Come in. I have told this gentleman all I had to say to him." He put his finger on his lips and looked at me. "This is for you, my friend," continued he, returning to the table, and taking a sealed letter from it ; "here are your instructions. If I should be unfortunate, read this, and pray do what I have requested of you."

"To the very letter! You have taken upon yourself to furnish the weapons?" asked the Baron Giordano, "are they in the carriage?"

"Yes," replied I, "but just when I was ready to leave home, I noticed that one of the hammers did not work well. We will take a box of pistols at Devisme's, as we pass there."

Louis looked at me with a smile, and offered me his hand. He seemed to understand that I did not wish him to be killed with one of my pistols.

"Have you a carriage," said Louis, "or shall Joseph go out and get one ?"

"I have my *coupé*," said the Baron, "and if we press a little, we can all three sit very well ; besides, as we are rather behind our time, we will be able to go quicker with my horses than with hacks."

"Let us go, then," said Louis.

We went down to the door. Joseph was waiting for us.

"Shall I go with monsieur?" asked he.

"No, Joseph, that's unnecessary, I shall not need you."

Then remaining a little behind—

"Here, my friend," said he, putting a small rouleau of gold into his hand, "if sometimes in my moments of ill humor I have offended you, pardon me."

"Oh! monsieur!" exclaimed Joseph, his eyes filling with tears, "what do you mean?"

"Hush!" said Louis, and advancing rapidly to the carriage, he placed himself between us.

"He was a good servant," said he, throwing a last look at Joseph, and if either of you can be useful to him, I shall feel very grateful for it."

"Do you dismiss him?" asked the Baron.

"No," said Louis, smiling, "I leave him, that's all."

We stopped at Devisme's door, and had barely time to take a box of pistols, powder and bullets; we then started again at the greatest speed of our horses.

We arrived at Vincennes at five minutes to nine. Another carriage arrived at the same moment as ours. It was Monsieur de Château-Renaud's. We entered the forest by two different roads, our drivers having received orders to join each other in the great alley.

In a few minutes we were at the place of rendezvous.

"Gentlemen," said Louis, while alighting, "you know no arrangement is possible."

"But, however," said I.

"Oh! *mon cher*, remember, that after the confidence I have reposed in you, you have less than any one else the right to propose or receive any."

I bowed my head before this absolute

determination, which seemed to me like a supreme will.

We left Louis near the carriage and advanced towards M. de Boissy and de Châteaugrand. Baron Giordano carried the box of pistols.

We exchanged a salute.

"Gentlemen," said the Baron, " in circumstances like these in which we find ourselves placed, the shortest compliments are the best, for every moment we may be interrupted. We have taken it upon us to furnish the weapons; here they are. Please to examine them. We have just got them from the gunsmith's, and give you our word that M. de Franchi has not even seen them."

"This assurance is unnecessary, sir," replied the Viscount de Châteaugrand, "we know with whom we have to do; and taking one pistol, while Mons. de Boissy took the other, the two seconds tried the play of the springs and examined the calibre of them.

"They are common target pistols," said the Baron, and have never been used. "Now, shall we have the liberty or not of using the double trigger?"

"But," said M. de Boissy, " my opinion is, that every one should do as he pleases, or as he is accustomed to do."

"Be it so," replied Giordano. "All equal chances are agreeable."

"You then inform Mons. de Franchi, and we will tell Mons. de Château-Renaud."

"That's all right now, sir. We have brought the pistols," continued Giordano, " and you must load them."

The two gentlemen each took a pistol, measured rigorously the same quantity of powder, took at random two bullets, put them into the barrels, and rammed them down.

During this operation, in which I had not wished to take an active part, I

went up to Louis, who received me with a smile.

"You will forget nothing that I have asked of you?" said he. "Obtain a promise from Giordano, that he will not mention any thing to my mother or brother. However, I have already made this request to him in the letter I gave him. See to it also, that the papers do not speak of it, or if they do, that no names are mentioned."

"You have, then, still the horrible conviction that you will be killed in this duel?" asked I.

"I am more certain of it than ever. But you will at least give me the credit of having beheld the approach of death like a true Corsican?"

"Your calmness, my dear de Franchi, is so grand, that it makes me hope that you are not fully convinced yourself."

Louis took out his watch.

"I have yet seven minutes to live," said he; "look here, this is my watch, keep it, I pray you, as a souvenir of me; it is an excellent *Brequet*."

I took the watch and pressing de Franchi's hand,

"In eight minutes," said I, " I hope to give it back to you."

"Let us not speak any more of that," replied he, " the gentlemen are approaching."

"Gentlemen," said the Viscount de Châteaugrand, "there must be somewhere about here a glade, which I have used on my own account last year. Shall we seek it? We would be much better there than in a lane, where we could be seen and disturbed."

"Guide us, sir," said Giordano; "we follow you."

The viscount walked first, we following, forming two separate groups. Indeed we soon found ourselves, after a gentle descent of about thirty steps,

5

in the middle of a glade, which had no doubt formerly been a pond like that of Auteuil, and which being entirely dried up formed a sort of bog, surrounded on all sides by a gentle slope.

The ground seemed, therefore, expressly made to serve as the theatre of the scene which was about to take place here.

" Monsieur de Martelli," said the viscount, " will you measure the steps with me ?"

The baron answered by bowing an affirmative ; then placing himself alongside of M. de Châteaugrand, they measured twenty ordinary steps.

I was left a few seconds longer alone with de Franchi.

" Apropos," said he, " you will find my will on the table, where I was writing when you came in."

" Very well, replied I, be easy."

" Gentlemen, whenever you please," said the Viscount de Châteaugrand.

" I am ready," said Louis. Then turning to me with a sad and melancholy smile, " Farewell ! my dear friend," continued he, " accept my thanks for all the trouble I have given you, and for that which I may yet occasion you."

I took hold of his hand, it was cold but not agitated.

" Well now," said I, " forget the vision of last night, and take the best aim you can."

" Do you recollect the *Freischutz* ?"

" Yes."

" Well then, you know that each bullet has its destination. Farewell !"

He met on his way the Baron de Giordano, who held in his hand the pistol which was destined for him. He took it, cocked it, and without even looking at it, went and took his position at the spot indicated by a handkerchief.

Mons. de Château-Renaud was already in his place.

There was a moment of grave silence, during which the two opponents saluted, first their own seconds, then the seconds of their adversary, and lastly each other.

Mons. de Château-Renaud appeared to be perfectly accustomed to this kind of affairs, and he smiled, like a man sure of his own skill. Besides, he knew perhaps, that this was the first time that Louis de Franchi had ever handled a pistol.

Louis was calm and cold ; his fine head looked like a marble bust.

" Well, gentlemen," said Château-Renaud, " you see we are waiting."

Louis gave me a last look, and then with a smile raised his eyes to heaven.

" Allons! gentlemen," said Châteaugrand, " prepare !"

Then clapping his hands together, cried out,

" One—two—three."

The two shots gave only one report. At the same moment I saw Louis de Franchi turn himself round twice and fall on his knee.

Mons. de Château-Renaud remained upright ; the facing of his coat only was shot through.

I rushed up to Louis.

" You are wounded !" exclaimed I.

He tried to answer me, but in vain ; a bloody foam appeared upon his lips. At the same time he let the pistol fall, and brought his hand up to the right side of his breast.

A hole, hardly large enough to admit the tip of the little finger, was visible in his overcoat.

" Baron," cried I, " run to the barrack and bring the surgeon of the regiment here."

But de Franchi summoning all his remaining strength, stopped Giordano, by making a sign with his head that it was unnecessary.

At the same time he fell upon his other knee.

Mons. de Château-Renaud left the place immediately, but the seconds approached the wounded man.

Meanwhile we had unbuttoned his overcoat and torn his vest and shirt open.

The bullet had entered under the sixth rib, on the right side, and gone out a little above the left hip.

At each respiration of the dying sufferer, the blood gushed out of the two wounds.

It was evident that the shot was fatal.

"Monsieur de Franchi," said the Viscount de Châteaugrand, "I assure you we are all of us exceedingly sorry for the result of this unfortunate affair, and we hope you have no hatred against M. de Château-Renaud."

"Yes, yes," murmured the wounded man, "yes, I pardon him—but make him go—make him go."

Then turning towards me,

"Remember your promise," said he.

"Oh! I swear to you, that all shall be done as you have desired."

"And now," said he smiling, "look at the watch."

And he fell back, uttering a sigh!

It was his last.

I looked at the watch, it was just ten minutes past nine.

I then cast my eyes upon Louis de Franchi: he was dead.

We took the body home with us, and while the Baron de Giordano went to make the necessary notification to the commissary of police of the quarter,

with the assistance of Joseph I carried it up into his room.

The poor fellow wept scalding tears.

When I entered the room, my eyes involuntarily were turned towards the *pendule*. It pointed at ten minutes after nine.

No doubt he had forgotten to wind it up, and it had stopped just at this time.

A moment after, Baron Giordano entered accompanied by the officers of justice, who, informed by him, came to put their seals on his effects.

Giordano spoke of sending letters of information to the friends and acquaintances of the deceased.

But I requested him first to read the letter, which Louis de Franchi had given him before we started.

The letter contained a solemn charge to conceal from his brother the cause of his death. Moreover, in order that no one should be admitted into the secret, he requested Giordano to arrange the funeral himself, as privately as possible.

Baron Giordano charged himself with all these details; and I went immediately to make a double visit to M. de Boissy and M. de Châteaugrand, to beg them to be silent on this unfortunate affair, and to request Mons. de Château-Renaud to leave Paris, at least for a short time, but without telling him for what reason his absence was solicited.

They both promised to assist as much as lay in their power, in the accomplishment of my wishes: and while they were on their way to see Mons. de Château-Renaud on the subject, I went to the post-office to despatch the letter which informed Madame de Franchi, that her son had died of a brain fever.

CHAPTER X.

Contrary to the usual custom with these affairs, the duel made but little noise. The papers even, those loud and false trumpets of publicity, kept silent. A few intimate friends only followed the corpse of the unfortunate young man to *Père-Lachaise.*

As to Monsieur de Château-Renaud, notwithstanding all the requests made to him, he refused to leave Paris.

For some time I indulged in the idea of following Louis' letters to his family with one from myself: for, although his object was excellent, this untruth on the occasion of the death of a son and brother was exceedingly repugnant to me. I was convinced that Louis himself had for a long time struggled against it, and that finally he had considered the important reasons which he had given me, necessary to decide him.

I therefore concluded, at the risk even of being accused of indifference and ingratitude, to keep silent on the subject; and I was convinced that Baron Giordano would do the same.

Five days after this occurrence, at about eleven o'clock in the evening, I was sitting at my table writing, near the chimney, alone and in low spirits, when my servant came in, shut the door carefully behind him, and in a very agitated voice told me that Monsieur de Franchi wished to see me.

I turned round and looked at him; he was extremely pale.

"What do you say, Victor?" asked I.

"Yes, indeed, sir," replied he, "I don't understand it myself."

"Of which Monsieur de Franchi do you speak?"

"But of your friend, sir; of the one whom I have seen once or twice coming here to see you."

"You are insane, fellow! Don't you know that he has unfortunately been killed five days ago?"

"Yes, sir, I do; and that is just the very reason why you see me so much disturbed. He rang the bell; I was in the anti-chamber. I opened the door, but recoiled upon seeing him. He then entered and asked if you were in. I was so much troubled that I told him you were; he then said, 'Go and inform your master that Monsieur de Franchi wishes to speak to him.' And lo, I am here."

"You are a fool, my friend. The anti-chamber was no doubt badly lighted, and you have seen wrong. You were half asleep and have not heard well. Return, and ask his name a second time."

"Oh! sir, that's useless. I swear to you that I have not been mistaken. I have both seen and heard perfectly well."

"Well, then, let him come in."

Victor returned to the door, trembling all over, and opened it, remaining in my room.

"Will the gentleman please to walk in?" said he.

I heard, indeed, in spite of the thick carpet, steps coming through the *salon,* and approaching my room. Immediately after, I saw in reality Monsieur de Franchi appear at the door.

I confess that my first feeling was that of terror. I rose up and took a step back.

"Excuse me for disturbing you at this hour," said Monsieur de Franchi, "but I arrived in the city about ten minutes ago, and you will easily understand that I did not wish to delay my conversation with you till to-morrow."

"Oh! my dear Lucien," exclaimed I, rushing up to him, and clasping him in my arms. "Is it you? Ah! it is you!"

And in spite of myself some tears escaped from my eyes.

"Yes," said he, "it is I."

I calculated the time that had elapsed; the letter could hardly have arrived at Ajaccio, and much less at Sullacaro.

"Good God!" exclaimed I, "but then you know nothing."

"I know all!" said he.

"How! all?"

"Yes."

",Victor," said I to my servant, who had not yet fully recovered, "leave us alone, or rather come in again in a quarter of an hour with a complete supper. You will sup with me, and stay over night, Lucien?"

"I accept all that," said Lucien, "I have not eaten since I left Auxerre. After that, as nobody knew me, or rather," continued he with a smile profoundly sad, "as every body seemed to recognize me at my poor brother's house, they did not admit me, and I left there after having thrown the whole house into confusion."

"Indeed, my dear Lucien, your resemblance to your brother Louis is so great, that I myself just now have been struck with it."

"How!" exclaimed Victor, who could not take his eyes off from him long enough to get out, "that gentleman is then the brother of ——"

"Yes; but go and get our supper."

Victor went out, and we were left alone. I took Lucien by the hand, led him to an arm-chair, and sat down beside him.

"But," continued I, still more and more astonished when I looked at him, "you were then on your way hither when you heard the fatal news?"

"No; I was at Sullacaro."

5*

"Impossible! Your brother's letter can hardly have reached there yet."

"Have you forgotten Burger's ballad, my dear Alexander? the *dead go quick.*"

I shuddered.

"What do you mean? explain yourself. I don't understand you."

"Have you forgotten what I told you about the apparitions peculiar to our family?"

"You have seen your brother?"— exclaimed I.

"Yes."

"And when was that?"

"During the night, from the 16th to the 17th."

"And he has told you all?"

"All!"

"He told you that he had died?"

"No. He told me that he had been *killed!* The dead never lie."

"And did he tell you how?"

"In a duel."

"By whom?"

"By Monsieur de Château-Renaud!"

"No! no! it cannot be," exclaimed I, "you have heard all this some other way; by some other means?"

"Do you think I am disposed to jest on this subject?"

"Pardon me: but what you now tell me is so strange, and indeed all that happens to you and your brother is so much out of the course of nature—"

"That you don't want to believe it! I understand. But look here," said he, opening his shirt and showing me a blue mark imprinted on his skin, above the sixth rib on the right side, "will you believe in that?"

"Indeed," exclaimed I, "that is exactly the spot where your brother received the fatal bullet!"

"And the bullet went out here," continued he, putting his finger above the left hip.

" That's miraculous!" cried I.

" And now," continued he, " will you permit me to tell you at what hour he died?"

" Speak!"

" At ten minutes past nine."

" Look.here, Lucien, tell me all at once, my mind grows confused with questioning you and listening to your incredible answers. I like a narration better."

" Ah! that will be very simple. The day on which my brother was killed, I had gone out early in the morning on horseback; I was visiting our shepherds near Carboni; when, after having looked at my watch, and just while I was putting it in my pocket, I received such a violent blow on my side that I fainted. When I opened my eyes, I was lying in Orlandini's arms, who was bathing my face with water. My horse was standing near, with his nose pointed towards me, blowing and snuffing.

" ' Well, said he, ' what has happened to you?'

" Oh!" replied I, " I do n't know myself; but did you not hear the report of fire-arms?

" ' No.'

" It appeared to me as if I had received a bullet here,—and I showed him the place where I felt the pain.

" ' First,' said he, ' there has not been a gun nor a pistol fired off in this neighborhood; and then you have no hole in your coat.'

" Then," replied I, " my brother has been killed."

" ' Ah!' exclaimed he, ' that's another thing.'

" I opened my coat and found the mark which I have shown you awhile ago. Only then it was fresh as if it was bleeding.

" For a moment I was unable to return to Sullacaro, so much had the double moral and physical pain I felt, affected me;.I thought of my mother, she expected me home to supper; I would then have had to explain to her a circumstance which I felt unable to do. For I did not wish, without further proof, to announce to her the death of my brother.

" I therefore continued my ride, and did not come home until six o'clock in the evening.

" My poor mother received me as usual; it was evident she did not suspect any thing. Soon after supper I retired to my room.

" In passing through the corridor, which you must recollect, the wind blew my candle out. I was going down stairs to light it again, when through the crevice of the door, I saw a light in my brother's room.

" I thought Griffo had had some business in that room, and had probably forgotten to take the light away.

" I pushed open the door; a wax taper was burning near my brother's bed, and on the bed my brother was lying naked and bloody.

" I confess, for a moment I remained struck with terror. I then approached and touched him, he was already cold.

" He had received a bullet through his body, in the same place where I had felt the pain, and a few drops of blood fell from the purple lips of the wound.

" I was now sure that my brother had been killed.

" I threw myself on my knees, and leaning my head on the bed, shut my eyes and murmured a prayer.

" When I opened my eyes again, I was in the most profound obscurity; the wax taper was extinguished, and the vision had disappeared.

" I felt the bed, it was empty.

"I consider myself as brave as any body else, but I must confess that when I left the room, groping in the dark, my hair stood upright and my brow was covered with sweat.

"I went down stairs to procure another light; my mother saw me, and uttered a cry.

"'What is the matter with you,' said she, 'why are you so pale?'

"Nothing, replied I, and taking another light I went up stairs again.

"This time the light did not go out, and I went into my brother's room. It was empty.

"On the floor I found my first candle, which I lighted.

"Notwithstanding this absence of new proofs, I had enough to convince me that my brother had been killed at ten minutes after nine o'clock.

"I retired to my room, and went to bed.

"As you may easily imagine, it was a long time before I could fall asleep. At length fatigue vanquished my agitation, and sleep overcame me.

"Then, all continued in the form of a dream; I saw the scene as it had occurred. I saw the man who has killed my brother, and heard his name pronounced; it was Mons. de Chateau-Renaud."

"Alas! all that is too true," exclaimed I, "but what is your object in coming to Paris?"

"I come to kill the man who has destroyed my brother."

"To kill him?"

"Oh! do n't be uneasy; not after the Corsican fashion, from behind a hedge, or over a wall. No, no, but after the French manner, with white gloves, a shirt frill and ruffles."

"And Madame de Franchi! does she know that you have come here with this intention?"

"Yes."

"And did she not object to your going?"

"She kissed me on the forehead, and said 'go!' My mother is a true Corsican."

"And then you started?"

"Here I am."

"But in his lifetime your brother did not wish to be revenged?"

"Well," said Lucien, smiling bitterly, "he has then changed his mind since he died."

At this moment the servant came in with the supper. We sat down, Lucien eating like a man whose mind was not at all pre-occupied. After supper I took him to his chamber, he thanked me, pressed my hand, and wished me good night."

This was the calmness which, in strong souls, follows a resolution firmly taken.

The following morning he came into my room as soon as the servant told him I was visible.

"Will you," said he, "accompany me to Vincennes? it is a pious pilgrimage I intend to make; if you have not time, I will go alone."

"How! by yourself, and who would show you the place?"

"Oh! I shall easily recognize it; did I not tell you I had seen it in my dream!"

I was curious to know how far this singular intuition would go.

"Very well, I will accompany you," said I.

"Get ready, then, while I am writing to Giordano. Will you permit me the use of your servant to carry this note to him?"

"With pleasure."

"Thank you."

He then went out, but returned in a

few minutes. In the meanwhile I had sent for a cab : we got into it and started for Vincennes.

On arriving at the cross-way,

"We are near the place, are we not ?" said Lucien.

"Yes, about twenty steps from here, on the right, we entered the forest."

"Here it is," said the young man, stopping the cab."

It was indeed the very spot.

Lucien entered the woods without any hesitation, as if he had been here twenty times. He walked straight up to the bog ; on arriving there he stopped for an instant, and looking round with a sort of instinctive familiarity, advanced directly to the spot where his brother had fallen. He bent his head to the ground ; and observing a reddish mark,

"Here it is!" said he.

He then touched the grass with his lips.

Then rising suddenly, his eyes flashing fire, he walked the whole length of the bog, till he came to the spot where Mons. de Château-Renaud had stood when he fired.

"Here he was standing," exclaimed he, stamping with his foot, and here you'll see him lie to-morrow."

"How!" cried I, "to-morrow?"

"Yes, unless he is a coward, he will give me my revenge to-morrow."

"But, my dear Lucien," said I, "you know that it is customary in France for a duel to produce no other consequences than those naturally arising from the duel itself. Monsieur de Château-Renaud has fought with your brother, whom he had challenged, but he has nothing to do with you."

"Ah! indeed! Mons. de Château-Renaud has had the right to challenge my brother because he offered his protection to a lady whom he had cowardly deceived! Mons. de Château-Renaud has killed my brother, who had never touched a pistol ; he has killed him with as much security as if he had shot at that roe buck, now looking at us. And I,—I,—I should not have the right to challenge Mons. de Château-Renaud ? Go,—go!"

I bent my head without answering.

"Besides," said he, "you have nothing to do with all this. Be easy, I have written to Giordano this morning, and by the time we get back to Paris, all the arrangements will be made. Do you think that Mons. de Château-Renaud would possibly refuse my proposition ?"

"Mons. de Château-Renaud has unfortunately a reputation for courage, which does not admit a doubt on this subject."

"Then all is for the best," said Lucien." "Let us go to breakfast."

We went back to the road, and got into the cab.

"Driver," said I, "Rue de Rivoli."

"No," said Lucien, "you are my guest. Driver, to the *Café de Paris*. Is it not there my brother usually took his meals ?"

"I believe so."

"Besides, I have told Giordano to meet us there."

"Well then, to the *Café de Paris*."

In about half an hour we alighted at the door of the Restaurant.

Lucien's *entrée* was a new proof of the astonishing resemblance between him and his brother. The circumstance of Louis' death had become known, not in all its particulars, it is true, but it was known, and Lucien's appearance here seemed to strike every body with an amazement almost stupifying.

I asked for a private cabinet, and left orders for the Baron Giordano to be shown into it, immediately on his arrival.

We were ushered into a room at the lower end of the *salon.* Lucien began to read the papers, with a calmness which looked like insensibility. When we were about half through our breakfast, Giordano came in.

The two young men had not seen each other for four or five years, notwithstanding which, a pressure of their hands was the only demonstration of friendship which they gave each other.

" Well, all is arranged !" said Giordano.

" Mons. de Chœteau-Renaud has accepted ?"

" Yes, but on condition, that after this he will be left unmolested."

" Oh! he may rest assured of it. I am the last of the de Franchi! Have you seen him or his seconds?"

" I saw him. He has offered himself to inform Mons. de Boissy as well as Mons. de Chateaugrand. As for the weapons, time and place, they will all be the same."

" Excellent! Take that seat and eat your breakfast."

The baron sat down, and we spoke of other things. After breakfast Lucien requested me to make him known to the commissary of police who had put on the seals, and also to the proprietor of the house where his brother had lived. He wished to pass in Louis' chamber the last night that separated him from his vengeance.

All these different arrangements took up the greater part of the day; and it was not until five o'clock in the afternoon that Lucien could take possession of the residence of his unfortunate brother.

We left him alone. Grief has a bashfulness, which demands respect.

Lucien gave me a rendezvous for the following morning at eight o'clock; he requested me to try to get the same pistols, and to buy them if they were for sale.

I went immediately to Devisme and the bargain was soon concluded, for six hundred francs.

The following morning, at a quarter before eight, I was at Lucien's door.

When I came in, he was sitting in the same place, and writing on the same table where I had found his brother similarly engaged.

He had a smile on his lips, though he looked very pale.

" Good morning," began he; " I am writing to my mother."

" I hope you will make her a less painful communication, than that which your brother made eight days ago."

" I inform her that she can now quietly pray for her son, and that he is avenged."

" How can you speak with so much certainty ?"

" Did not my brother announce his death to you, beforehand ? I, in advance, now assure you of the death of Mons. de Chàteau-Renaud. Look here !" said he, rising and touching my temple, I shall lodge the bullet there."

" And you ?"

" He will not even touch me !"

" But at least wait till after the duel, before you despatch this letter."

" That 's altogether useless."

He rung the bell. The servant entered.

" Joseph," said he, " take this letter to the post-office."

" You have then seen your brother ?" cried I.

" Yes," replied Lucien.

It was a strange thing indeed, these two duels following one after the other, and in both of which, one of the adversaries was beforehand doomed to die.

Meanwhile, Baron Giordano arrived. It was eight o'clock. We started.

Lucien was so anxious to get there, and hurried the driver on so much, that we arrived at the rendezvous ten minutes before the time. Our opponents came up at nine o'clock precisely. They were all three on horseback, followed by a servant, mounted also. Mons. de Château-Renaud held his hand in the breast of his coat, and I thought at first that he carried his arm in a sling.

At twenty steps from us, the three gentlemen dismounted, leaving their horses to the care of the servant.

Mons. de Château-Renaud staid behind, but remained looking over at Lucien; notwithstanding the distance between us, I saw him grow pale. He turned back, and amused himself with cutting down the small flowers in the grass with his whip, which he carried in his left hand.

"Here we are, gentlemen," said M. M. de Châteaugrand and de Boissy, "but you know our conditions, that is, that this duel shall be the last, and that whatever may be the result, Mons. de Château-Renaud shall not incur any further responsibility."

"Agreed!" replied we.

Lucien bowed in sign of his approbation.

"You have weapons?" inquired the viscount.

"Yes; the same used the other day."

"And they are unknown to Mons. de Franchi?"

"Much more so than to Mons. de Château-Renaud, who has used them once. Mons. de Franchi has not even seen them."

"Very well, gentlemen. Come, Château-Renaud."

We immediately entered the woods without uttering a single word. Each one felt a painful recollection of the recent scene, upon the theatre of which we were soon to appear, and where something not less terrible would probably occur.

We arrived at the bog.

Mons. de Château-Renaud, by a great effort of self-control, appeared calm. But it was easy for those who had seen him at both *rencontres*, to distinguish the difference in his feelings.

From time to time he cast a glance at Lucien, which expressed an uneasiness, that looked very much like fear. Perhaps it was the great likeness of the two brothers which occupied him, or did he see in Lucien the avenging shadow of Louis?

At length, while the pistols were being loaded, I saw him take his hand out of his breast; it was enveloped in a wet handkerchief, in order to subdue its feverish motion.

Lucien was waiting, with his eyes calm and fixed, like one sure of vengeance.

Without being shown to his place, Lucien took his stand on the spot which his brother had occupied, and of course forced M. de Château-Renaud to take again the same place where he had stood before.

Lucien received his pistol with a joyful smile.

When Mons. de Château-Renaud took his, from being pale, he became livid. He then passed his hand between his neck and his cravat, as if the latter had been choking him.

It is impossible to imagine the feeling of involuntary terror with which I regarded this young man: beautiful, rich, elegant, who but the previous morning had seen long years of happiness before him, and who now, the sweat pouring from his forehead and his heart filled with unutterable agony, felt himself fated to die.

"Are you ready?" demanded the Viscount Châteaugrand.

"Yes," replied Lucien.

Mons. de Château-Renaud merely made a sign in the affirmative.

As for myself, I turned away.

I heard the two claps of the hands given successively, and with the third, the report of the two pistols.

I turned round again. Monsieur de Château-Renaud was lying prostrate upon the ground, quite dead, without having uttered a sigh, or made a movement. I went up to him, impelled by that invincible curiosity which urges us to follow a catastrophe to the end. The bullet had entered the temple, at the very spot predicted by Lucien the day before.

I ran up to him; he had remained calm and motionless. But upon seeing me within his reach, he dropped his pistol and threw himself into my arms.

"Oh! my brother! my poor brother!" exclaimed he.

He broke out into sobs!

These were the first tears the young man had ever shed!